MASTERS OF THE PIT

Masters of the Pit

MICHAEL MOORCOCK

NEW ENGLISH LIBRARY
TIMES MIRROR

For Mr. Chip Delany of San Francisco and
Sister Mary Eugene of Bon Secours Convent,
Derby, Pennsylvania

... the sickness is Fear and the remedy is Faith ...

First published in Great Britain by Compact Books
© 1969 by Michael Moorcock

*

FIRST NEL PAPERBACK EDITION JULY 1971

*N E L Books are published by The New English Library Limited, from Barnard's
Inn, Holborn, London, E.C.1. Made and printed in Great Britain at The Philips
Park Press Manchester*

450007219

INTRODUCTION

SITTING in my study one autumn night, a small fire burning in the grate taking the chill off a room filled with the scents of oncoming winter, I heard a footfall in the hall below.

I am not a nervous man, but I can be an imaginative one, and I had thoughts of both ghosts and burglars as I left the leather armchair and opened the door. The hall was quiet and the lights were out, but I saw a shadowy figure coming up the stairs towards me.

There was something about the size of the man, something about the jingle he made as he walked, that I recognized instantly. A grin began to spread across my face as he approached, and I held out my hand to him.

"Michael Kane?" It was hardly a question.

"It is," replied the deep, vibrant voice of my visitor. He came to the top of the stairs and I felt my hand enclosed in a firm, manly grip. I saw the giant smile in return.

"How is Mars?" I asked, as I led him into the study.

"A little changed from when we last spoke," he said.

"You must tell me," I said eagerly. "What will you have to drink?"

"No liquor, thanks. I'm not used to it any longer. How about some coffee? That's the one thing I miss on Mars."

"Wait here," I told him. "I'm all alone in the house today. I'll go and make some."

I left him slumped in a chair beside the fire, his magnificent, bronzed body completely relaxed. He looked strangely incongruous in his Martian war harness, studded as it was with unfamiliar gems, his huge longsword with its ornate basket hilt resting with its tip on the floor.

His diamond-blue eyes seemed much more humorous and even less full of tension than when I had last seen him. His manner had relaxed me, too, even in my excitement at seeing my friend again.

In the kitchen I prepared the coffee, remembering all that

he had told me of his past adventures – of Shizala, Princess of the Varnala and of Hool Haji, now ruler of Mendishar, his wife and his closest friend respectively I remembered how his first trip to Mars* – an ancient Mars, far in our own past – had been made accidentally because of a malfunctioning matter transmitter, a development of laser research he had been pursuing in Chicago; how he had met and fought for Shizala against the fearsome Blue Giants and their leader Horguhl, a woman of her own race who had a secret power over people, across the lush landscapes of a strange planet. I remembered how he had sought my help and I had given it – building a matter transmitter in my own basement. He had returned to Mars** and had faced many dangers, discovering the lost underground city of the Yaksha, helping to win a revolution and fighting strange, spider creatures before finally finding Shizala again and marrying her. Using the forgotten scientific devices of the Yaksha – a race now supposed to be extinct – he had built a machine capable of flinging him across Time and Space again to a transceiver in my basement.

Evidently he had, as he had promised before he left the last time, returned to tell me of his latest adventures.

I went back with the coffee and set it in front of him.

He poured himself a cup, tasting it a little suspiciously at first, then added milk and sugar. He took his first swallow and grinned.

"One thing I haven't lost my taste for," he said.

"And one thing I haven't lost *my* taste for," I replied eagerly. "I want to hear your latest story from beginning to end."

"Have you published the first two adventures yet?" he asked.

At that time I had not, so I shook my head. "Someone will believe me sufficiently to publish them," I told him. "People believe I wrote them cynically for one reason or another – but we know that I did not, that you are real, that your exploits actually happened. One day they will realize this, when governments are prepared to release the information that confirms what you have told me. They will realize that you are no

*(See 'City of the Beast' – NEL, 1971)
**(See 'Lord of the Spiders' – NEL, 1971)

liar and that I am no crack-pot – or worse, a commercial writer trying to write a science fiction novel."

"I hope so," he said seriously, "because it would be a shame for people not to be able to read the story of my experiences on Mars."

As he finished his first cup of coffee and reached forward to help himself to another, I fixed the tape-recorder so that it would take down every word he said. Then I settled back in my chair.

"Is your marvellous memory working at full capacity as usual?" I asked.

He smiled. "I think so."

"And you're going to tell me of your recent adventures on Mars?"

"If you wish to hear them."

"I do. How is Shizala, your wife? How is Hool Haji, your friend the Blue Giant? And Horguhl – any news of her?"

"None of Horguhl," he said. "And Fate be thanked for that!"

"Then what? Surely things can't have been so uneventful on Mars!"

"They certainly were not. I am only just recovering from everything that happened. Telling you about it all will help me, as usual, to bring it into perspective. Where shall I begin?"

"The last I heard from you was that you and Shizala were living happily in Varnal, that you had designed airships to supplement the Varnalian air force, and that you had made several expeditions to the Yaksha underground city to study their machines."

"That's right." He nodded thoughtfully. "Well, I can begin with our sixth expedition to the Yaksha city. That was when things really started to happen. Are you ready?"

"I am ready," I replied.

Kane began his story.

EPB
Chester Square,
London, S.W.1.
August 1969

Chapter One

THE AERIAL EXPEDITION

I KISSED Shizala farewell, little realizing that I would not see her again for many Martian months, and clasped the ladder leading into the cabin of my airship – a vessel designed to my own specifications.

Shizala looked lovelier than ever, a womanly woman who was, without doubt, the most beautiful human being on the whole planet of Mars.

The slender towers of Varnal, the city of which I was now a Bradhinak, or prince, rose around us in the light of the early morning sun. There was a smell of scented mist – the green mist which came from the lake in the centre of Varnal, sending delicate green traceries through the air to mingle with the pennants of lovely colours floating at masts rising from the towers. Most of the buildings are tall and white, though a number are of fine blue marble, while others have veins of gold running through them. It is a delicate, beautiful city – perhaps the finest on Mars.

This was where we had lived since our marriage and we had been exquisitely happy there. But I am a restless soul and my mind was eager for new information about the forgotten machines of Mars in the vaults of the Yaksha, which still needed investigation.

Thus, when Hool Haji had flown from Mendishar, far in the North, to visit me, it had not been long before I had suggested an expedition to the Yaksha vaults, partially for the sake of old times.

He had agreed eagerly, and so it had been decided. We should only be away for the equivalent of an Earthly week, and Shizala, loving me with a deep and abiding love which I fully reciprocated, did not object to this venture.

Now Hool Haji, the Blue Giant who had become my firmest friend on Mars, waited above in the cabin of the airship as it swayed gently in the breeze.

Once more I kissed Shizala without speaking. There was no need for speech – we communicated with our eyes, and that was sufficient.

I began to climb the ladder into the ship.

The interior was comfortably furnished with couches of a stuff rather like red plush, and the metal work was similar to brass and polished in the same way. There was something vaguely nostalgic and Victorian about the design and I had encouraged the motif throughout the ship. The ropes criss-crossing the gas-bag, for instance, were of thick, red cord and the metal cabin had been painted in bright greens and reds, with scroll-work picked out in gold. The controls of the ship were at the front, and once again these were of the brass-like metal, enamelled in black.

I started the engine as I climbed into the seat next to Hool Haji, whose massive, blue-skinned bulk dwarfed me.

My friend watched with interest as I pulled a lever, releasing the cords which held the ship near the ground, and I began to steer her away from Varnal – not without a pang, for I knew that I should miss both Shizala and the City of Green Mists.

I did not know then that I was to be separated from them for a very long time, that circumstances were so to arrange themselves that I would face death, endure enormous discomforts and experience hideous dangers before I should see them again.

It was, however, in this slightly melancholy mood, yet with mounting excitement at the prospect of studying the Yaksha machines again, that I set course Northwards. It was going to be a long journey, even in my comparatively speedy airship.

The journey to the Yaksha city in the desert was not to be without interruption, however, for on the second day of our trip the engines began to falter. I was surprised, for I trusted my engineers.

I turned to Hool Haji. My friend was looking down at the country far below. It was a predominantly yellow landscape, of great flowers similar to gigantic irises, swaying below us as if in a graceful, though monotonous, dance. Every so often the sea of yellow flowers was broken by effusions of blue or green,

10

each splash of colour, a bloom like a marigold in general appearance. Even at this distance above them, they sent up languorous scents that delighted my nostrils. Hool Haji seemed entranced by this beauty and had not even noticed the change of note in the engine.

"It looks as if we might have to land," I informed him.

He glanced up at me. "Why, Michael Kane? Would it not be unwise?"

"What do you mean, unwise?" I asked.

He pointed downwards.

"The flowers."

"We could find a clearing."

"That is not what I am trying to say. Have you not heard of the Flowers of Modnaf? They are attractive at a distance but highly dangerous when you come close to them. Their scent from here is pleasant, but when approached more closely it induces first a lethargy, then a creeping madness. Many have been trapped by these flowers and their vitality sapped, leaving them dry of everything human, to become mindless creatures wandering eventually to the quicksands of Golana, where they are sucked down slowly and never heard of again."

I shuddered. "No human being should suffer such a fate!"

"But many have! And those who have survived have become little more than walking dead men."

"Then let us steer a course away from both Modnaf and Golana and hope that our motor does not give up until they are far behind us," I said, making up my mind to avoid the dangers below us at all costs, even if it necessitated drifting in the wind until we had passed them by.

As I nursed the engine along, Hool Haji told me the story of an old, desperate man who had once dreamed of power, one Blemplac the Mad, who was still supposed to wander below. He had imbibed so much of the scents that they no longer affected him as they did others and he had managed to survive the quicksands – because he had been their original creator. Apparently he had once been a benevolent and beneficient man who had acquired a little scientific knowledge from somewhere and had dreamed of greatness. Knowing little of what he handled, he had tried to use his knowledge to build

11

a vast, gleaming tower that would inspire men with its beauty and grandeur. The foundations had been laid and it had seemed for a long time that he would succeed. Sadly, something had gone wrong and his mind had become affected. His experiment had gone out of control and the result was the quicksands, which had peculiar and unnatural properties found nowhere else.

At length, and with a feeling of tremendous relief, we passed over the flowers and the quicksands. I had only observed the quicksands at night, by the light of the moons that hurtled above, but the glimpse was enough to tell me that Hool Haji had not exaggerated. Strange cries had risen from the slowly shifting muck below, insane ravings that sometimes seemed to be words, but I could make no sense out of them, nor did I try very hard.

By morning we were crossing a series of deep, gleaming lakes dotted with green islands and the occasional boat scudding across the vast expanse of water.

I remarked on the welcome contrast to Hool Haji and he agreed. While we had crossed the previous territory he had been more disturbed than he had admitted. I asked if it was sensible to try to land, since the engine was now working in fits and starts and was soon bound to give up altogether. He said it would be safe, for these were the islands of enlightened and intelligent folk who had the ability to entertain and delight any visitor to the lakes. He pointed out names as we passed over them. There was one lush island, set somewhat apart from the rest.

"That is an island called Drallab," Hool Haji explained. "It's folk have only rare contact with their neighbours, but though they appear to play little part in the activities of the other islands they exert a great artistic influence on them and are really extremely benevolent. They entertained me once, when I travelled the islands, and I enjoyed every moment of my stay."

Another island appeared. This was a strange-looking place of peculiar contrasts for so small an island. I could make out a small forest, a mountain, a barren area and other features. This was K'cocroom, Hool Haji informed me, an island that had only in the last few years emerged from the lake and was still largely unpopulated, though the few people who lived there seemed a folk of strange contrasts, sometimes friendly to strangers, sometimes not.

We decided not to land there and passed over several other islands, with Hool Haji naming them all with great affection. There was S'Sidla, a gentle landscape of strong, straight trees and rich, dark glades, and Nosirrah, a rugged, healthy looking place with, Hool Haji informed me, great treasures yet unmined.

I was eager to hear all this, even though part of my attention was on the engine, for everything I heard told me more about a world I had still only partially explored, and the more I knew the better I would be equipped to survive in it.

At length we had managed to nurse the airship over all the islands and saw ahead of us on the mainland – which we decided was a better place to land in case the engine proved unrepairable – a city which was called, Hool Haji told me, Cend-Amrid. The people, he said, were well known for their craftsmanship and skill with the few technical devices in circulation on Mars. They would help us more than the islanders, though the islanders were possibly more friendly.

I manipulated my controls and we began to drop down towards Cend-Amrid.

Later I was to regret not landing on one of the islands, for Hool Haji was to find Cend-Amrid changed from the place he had known when, as a wandering outcast, he had spent some time in the city.

But it was with relief in our hearts that we drifted over the city as evening came, bathing its dark towers in deep shadow.

It was a silent place and few lights burned, but I put this down to the fact that its inhabitants were a hard-working folk, according to Hool Haji, whose pleasures were simple and did not extend to any kind of night-time festivities.

We descended on the outskirts of the city and I released the grappling anchor which imbedded its sharp prongs into the earth and enabled me to climb down the ladder and secure the ropes to a couple of stunted trees that grew nearby.

13

Chapter Two

CITY OF THE CURSE

As we walked towards Cend-Amrid, Hool Haji's hand went instinctively to his sword-hilt. Knowing him so well, I recognized the gesture and found it puzzling.

"Something wrong?" I asked.

"I am not sure, my friend," he said quietly.

"I thought you said Cend-Amrid would be a safe place for us."

"So I thought. But I am uneasy. I cannot explain it."

His mood conveyed itself to me and a trace of darkness clouded my brain.

Hool Haji shrugged. "I am tired. I expect that is all it is."

I accepted the explanation and we walked towards the gate of the city, feeling a little less perturbed.

The gate was open and no guards protected it. If the people were so generous-spirited to allow this, then this would mean we should have little difficulty in finding help.

Hool Haji, however, muttered something about this being unusual. "They are not a gregarious folk," he said.

Into the silent streets we walked. The tall, dark buildings seeming without a trace of life, like stage sets built for some extravagant production – and the stage seemed empty now.

Our feet echoed as we stepped along. Hool Haji leading the way towards the centre of the city.

A little later I heard something else and stopped, putting my hand on Hool Haji's arm.

We listened.

There it was – a soft footfall such as would be made by a man walking in cloth slippers or boots of very fine leather.

The sounds came towards us. Again Hool Haji's hand went instinctively to his sword-hilt.

Round the corner came a figure swathed in a black cloak, folded over his head to form a rudimentary hood. He held a

14

bunch of flowers in one hand and a large flat case in the other.

"Greetings," I said formally, in the Martian manner. "We are visitors to your city and seek help."

"What help can Cend-Amrid give to any human soul?" the swathed man muttered bleakly, and there was no note of interrogation in his voice.

"We know your folk to be practical and useful when dealing with machines. We thought ..." Hool Haji's statement was cut off when the man voiced a strange laugh.

"Machines! Speak not to me of machines!"

"Why so?"

"Do not stay to find out, strangers. Leave Cend-Amrid while you may!"

"Why should we not speak of machines? Has some taboo been imposed? Do the people hate machines now?" I knew that in some Earthly societies machines were feared and that popular thought rejected them since people feared their lack of humanity, that too much emphasis on automation and the like made some philosophers uneasy that human beings might become too artificial in their outlook, and that as a scientist on Earth I had sometimes encountered this attitude at parties where I had been accused of all sorts of wickedness because of my work concerning nuclear physics. I wondered if the folk of Cend-Amrid had taken this reaction to its ultimate conclusion and banned the machines some feared, and this was why I felt encouraged to ask the question.

But again the man laughed.

"No," he said. "People do not hate machines – unless they hate one another."

"Your remarks are obscure," I said impatiently. "What is wrong?" I was beginning to think that the first man we had met in Cend-Amrid was a madman.

"I have told you," he said – and his head turned and he glanced around him, as if he was nervous. "Do not stay to discover what is wrong. Leave Cend-Amrid at once. Do not remain a second longer. This is the city of the curse!"

Perhaps we should have taken his advice, but we did not. We stayed to argue, and that was to be, in the short-term, a mistake which we were to regret.

"Who are you?" I asked. "Why are you the only man abroad in Cend-Amrid?"

"I am a physician," he said. "Or *was*!"

"You mean you have been expelled from your physician's guild?" I suggested. "You are not allowed to practise?"

Again the laugh, infinitely bitter – a laugh that hovered on the brink of insanity.

"I have not been expelled from my guild. I am simply no longer a physician. I am known in these days as a Servicer of Grade 3 Types."

"What are these 'types' that you service? Are you a mechanic now, or what?"

"I am told to be a mechanic. I service human beings. These are the Grade 3 Types – human beings!" The words came out as a cry of misery. "I used to be a doctor – my whole training was to give me sympathy for my patients. And now I am" – he sobbed – "a mechanic. My job is to look at the human machine and decide if it can be made to function with minimum attention. If I decide that it cannot be made to function in this way, I must mark it down for scrapping and its parts go to a bank for use by the healthy machines."

"But this is monstrous!"

"It *is* monstrous," he said softly. "And now you must leave this cursed city immediately. I have said too much."

"But how did this situation arise?" Hool Haji asked insistently. "When I was last in Cend-Amrid the people seemed an ordinary, practical folk – dull, perhaps, but that is all."

"There is practicality," replied the physician, "and there is the human factor, the emotional factor in Man. Together they mean Man. But let one factor be encouraged and the other actively discouraged, and you have one of two ultimates – insofar as humanity is concerned."

"What are they?" I asked, interested in this argument in spite of myself.

"You have either the Beast or the Machine," he said simply.

"That seems an oversimplification," I said.

"So it is. But we are dealing with a society that has become oversimplified," he said, warming a little to his subject in spite of his nervous glances up and down the street. "Here the

Machine in Man has been encouraged and, if you like, it is the stupidity of the Beast which has encouraged it – for the Beast cannot predict and Man can. The Beast in Man leads him to create Machines for his well-being, and the Machine adds first to his comfort and then to his knowledge. In a healthy land this would all work together in the long run. But Cend-Amrid's folk cut themselves off from too much. Now Cend-Amrid is not a healthy place in any way whatsoever."

"But something must have caused all this. Some dictator must have brought this madness to Cend-Amrid," I said.

"The Eleven rule in Cend-Amrid – no one man dominates. But the dictator who holds sway over the city is the dictator who has always ruled mankind through the ages – unless the stories of the immortal Sheev are true."

"You speak of Death," I said.

"I do. And the form Death takes in Cend-Amrid is one of the most awesome."

"What is that?"

"Disease – a plague. The dictator Death brought fear – and fear led the Eleven to their doctrine."

"But what exactly *is* their doctrine?" Hool Haji asked.

The physician was about to reply when he suddenly drew in his breath with a hiss and began to scuttle back the way he had come.

"Go!" he whispered urgently as he fled. "Go now!"

His fear had so affected us that we were almost ready to obey his imperative when down the long, dark street towards us came an incredible sight.

It was like a giant sedan chair, a huge box with handles on all four lower sides, borne on the shoulders of some hundred men who moved as one. I had seen armies on the move, but even the most regimented detachment of soldiers had never moved with the fantastic precision of these men carrying the great box on their shoulders.

Seated in the box and visible through the unglazed windows on the two sides that were most clearly visible to me were two men. Their faces were immobile and their bodies stiff and straight. They did not look in any way alive – just as the men who bore this strange carriage did not look alive. This

17

was not a sight I had ever expected to see on Mars, where the human individual, no matter what battles and tensions arose in ordinary life, was respected and regimentation of the sort I now observed had hitherto seemed totally alien. Every instinct in me was outraged by the sight and tears of anger came into my eyes. Perhaps this was all instinctive then; perhaps I have rationalized my feelings since. But no matter. I was offended by the sight – deeply, emotionally and psychologically – and my reason was offended, too. What I saw was an example of the insanity the almost-insane physician had spoken of.

I could feel that Hool Haji, too, was offended in the same way, reacting against the sight.

Happily we are men of sense and controlled our instincts for the moment. It is a good thing to do this but a bad thing to use this control – which, as rational human beings, we have – to convince ourselves that action is never needed. We simply bided our time and I decided to learn more of this dreadful place before I began to work against it.

For work against it I was going to. That, I decided, there and then. If the cost was my life and all I held dear, I swore an oath to myself that I would eradicate the corruption that had come to Cend-Amrid, not only for my own sake but for the sake of all Mars.

I did not then, as the carriage approached us, understand to what ends I would be driven in order to carry out my personal vow. I did not realize the implications of my oath.

Even if I had it would not have diverted me from my path. The decision made, the vow sworn – and I sensed Hool Haji's own personal vow sworn, because he was my friend and because I knew just how much we had in common – I stood my ground and waited for the carriage to reach us.

Reach us it did, then it stopped.

One of the men leaned forward and in a cold voice, devoid of emotion, said:

"Why you come Cend-Amrid?"

I was momentarily taken aback by the form of the question. It went so well with the dead face.

18

Something in me made me reply in a more flowery manner than the one which I normally employ.

"We come with open hearts to ask a favour of the folk of Cend-Amrid. We come with nothing to offer but our gratitude, to ask you for help."

"What help?"

"We have a motor that is malfunctioning. A flying ship of my own construction with a motor of a kind unlikely to be found on Mars."

"What kind motor?"

"The principle is simple. I call it an internal combustion engine – but that will mean little to you."

"Does it work?"

"It is not working at present, and that is why we are here," I explained, quelling my impatience. The malfunctioning engine was decreasing in importance after what I had observed in the place that the physician had so aptly termed the City of the Curse.

"Do principles work well?" asked the dead-faced man.

"Normally," I replied.

"If it works it good, if not work then bad," came the emotionless voice.

"Can you work?" I said angrily, hating the implications of the questions.

"Cend-Amrid work."

"I mean – can you repair my motor?"

"Cend-Amrid do anything."

"Will you repair my motor?"

"Cend-Amrid think will repair of motor be good for Cend-Amrid?"

"It will be good for us – and therefore ultimately good for Cend-Amrid."

"Cend-Amrid must debate. You come."

"I think we'd prefer to stay outside, spend the night in our ship and learn your decision in the morning."

"No. Not good. You not known."

I was struck by the incredibly primitive reasoning of the man who spoke and saw at once to what the physician had

19

been referring when he mentioned the Beast creating the Machine and leaving Man out of it altogether. Perhaps, looking back, this was good for me, for I realize now exactly what my Mars means to me in logical terms. Make no mistake, the curse which had come to Cend-Amrid was even more alien to the Mars I love than it would be to Earth. And, perhaps because Mars was not prepared against the dangers inherent in Cend-Amrid, I felt that it was my duty to eradicate the disease as soon as possible.

"I think it would be best, however, if we left Cend-Amrid and waited outside," I said. It was my intention, of course, to try to repair the motor and get back to Varnal as soon as possible, there to get help. One part of me was aware that just as I resented an intrusion on my own personal liberty, the rulers of Cend-Amrid would resent an intrusion of mine, but the decision had been taken and in my heart I knew I was right, though I decided there and then that if violence could be avoided then it would be avoided, for I am fully aware that violence produces nothing, in the end, but further violence, and to react in terms of violence is only to create more violence in the future.

The dead-faced man's reply was, in fact, an illustration of this when he said:

"No. Best for Cend-Amrid you stay. If not stay then Cend-Amrid make stay."

"You will use force to make us stay?"

"Use many men make two men stay."

"That sounds like force to me, my friend," said Hool Haji with a grim smile, and his hand went to his sword. Again I stayed his arm.

"No, my friend – later, perhaps, but let us first see what we can of this place. With luck they will see no reason in not helping us. For the moment let us curb our emotions and go along with them." I muttered this rapidly and the dead-faced man, whose partner beside him had not moved or spoken at any time, did not appear to hear.

"For the moment," he growled.

"Only for the moment," I assured him.

The dead-faced man said: "Do you come?"

"We'll come," I said.

"Follow," he ordered, and then to the carriage-bearers, who had remained as expressionless and immobile as he and his friend, he said: "Bearers go back to Central Place."

Then came another horrifying and unexpected event.

Instead of turning round, the carriage-bearers began to run backwards.

Was this efficiency, even in the limited terms of the rulers of Cend-Amrid?

It was not. It was madness, pure and simple. Sight of this madness almost made me lose the control I had been fighting to maintain, but noticing Hool Haji's stance and knowing that he, too, was about to break, made me restrain him again and thus restrain myself.

In a mood of outraged horror that made me understand just why the physician had seemed insane we followed the carriage.

Chapter Three

THE ELEVEN

THE Central Place had obviously been created by careful calculation of the exact centre of Cend-Amrid, then knocking down existing buildings and putting up a structure that was square and squat, contrasting unnaturally with the other buildings. The Central Place also showed signs of having been erected only recently, and I marvelled at how speedily it must have been built and at what cost – since it must have been created primarily by human labour!

The Central Place had been built by the blood of men – man subjected to a tyranny far harder to understand than that created by some power-mad dictator!

The carriage stopped and was lowered to the ground outside the main entrance – a perfect square let into the side – and from it, walking like robots, the two men descended, leading the way into the building.

Inside it was dim, poorly illuminated by simple lamps that seemed roughly the same as our oil lamps. This surprised me since most Martian peoples still use the almost everlasting artificial lighting that was one of the benefits left behind by the Sheev – the super-scientific race that had, according to legend and the little history that remained, destroyed themselves in a monstrous war many centuries earlier, leaving just a few immortals who had learned the error of their ways and rarely became involved in the affairs of men, fearing perhaps that they might repeat their errors.

I remarked on this to Hool Haji and he said that they had once had these lights, but in attempting to make more like them had taken them all to pieces and hadn't been able to put them together again.

This information added to my impression of the people of Cend-Amrid and helped me to understand why they had become what they were. In sympathizing with the causes of their insanity, it did not alter one wit my intention to attempt, in the best way I could, to eradicate this insanity.

We walked behind the two into a chamber where we found nine more men, all having the same unnaturally erect bearing and immobile expression as the first two. They differed, of course, in physical appearance.

The first two took their places at a circular table where the other nine already sat. In the centre of the table, which had been hollowed out, was a grisly sight. In this place it seemed strange that it should be there – until I realized the exact significance of it.

It was a human skeleton.

A *memento mori*, in fact.

Originally – and perhaps even the Eleven had now lost sight of their original motive – it had been placed there to remind them of death. If the physician had been right, it was fear of the plague which had caused them to create this unnatural system of government.

The next thing I noticed was that there was one place short at the table. Yet if there were twelve seats around the skeleton, then where was the twelfth? For the rulers of Cend-Amrid called themselves the Eleven.

I hoped that I might find an answer to this later on.

In the same flat voice, the man I had originally spoken with told the other ten exactly what had passed between us. He made no personal comment on this and did not seem to be trying to convey anything but the precise information.

When he had finished, the others turned to regard us.

"We talk," said the first man after a moment.

"Shall we go, so that you can decide?" I asked.

"No need. We consider factors. You here not matter."

And then began an incredible conversation between the eleven men. Not once did anyone state an opinion depending on his own personality. To some this might sound attractive – reason ruling emotions – but to experience it was horrifying, for I suddenly realized that a man's personal point of view is necessary if any realistic conclusion is to be reached, no matter how imperfect it might seem.

To repeat the whole conversation would bore you but, in

essence, they debated whether by being of use to us they could get something good for Cend-Amrid.

Finally they came to a conclusion – a conclusion which I couldn't help feeling a more balanced human being would have come to in a matter of moments. Briefly, it was this: If I would explain how an internal combustion engine was constructed and explain, in general, how it worked, they would help me repair mine.

I knew how dangerous it could be if I started this unhealthy society on the road to real technical advancement, but I pretended to agree, knowing also that they did not have the tools necessary to build many internal combustion engines before I could be back with help and attempt to cure the sickness that had come to Cend-Amrid.

"You show?" queried one of the eleven.

"I show," I agreed.

"When?"

"In the morning."

"Morning. Yes."

"Can we now return to our airship?"

"No."

"Why not?"

"You stay, you not stay. We now know. So you stay here."

I shrugged. "Very well. Then perhaps we can sleep somewhere until the morning." At least, I thought, we could conserve our energy until we had decided how to act.

"Yes."

"Is there an inn we could stay at?"

"Yes, but you not stay there."

"Why not? You could guard it if you didn't trust us."

"Yes, but you die, not die. We not know. So you stay here."

"Why might we die?"

"Plague make die."

I understood. They did not want us to become infected with the plague, which still held sway, we gathered, in the city. This place was better protected, perhaps, than the rest of the city.

We agreed to stay.

The first man then led us out of the chamber and down a

24

short passage-way, at the end of which a flight of steps ran downwards into the cellars of the Central Place.

We descended the steps and came to another passage with many doors on both sides. They looked suspiciously like a row of cells in a prison.

I asked the man what they were.

"Malfunctioning heads kept here," he told me.

I knew then that this was probably where the people who were still useful to Cend-Amrid, in the city's terms, but who had been judged insane, again in the city's terms, were imprisoned.

Presumably we were thought to be in this class. So long as they did not remove our weapons I was willing to let them lock us up for the night if, by allowing this, we could eventually get our motor repaired and make the journey back to Varnal, there to decide how best we could overcome the double curse lying on Cend-Amrid – the curse of physical and mental disease. A combination, I could not help thinking, that was rare on Mars – where disease is rare – but far less so on Earth. Another thing I could not help considering was whether, if there had been more disease on Mars, the people would be the same. I concluded that they would not have been. I think I am right.

I am a scientist, I know, but I am not a philosophical man – I prefer action to thought. But the example of Cend-Amrid affected me deeply and I feel I must take pains to explain just why I prefer the society of Mars to the society of Earth. Mars, of course, is not perfect – and perhaps it is partially why I have found my true home on Mars. For there the people have learned the lesson of trying too hard for perfection. There, on the whole, they have learned the great lesson – to respect the human individual above all things. Not merely to respect the strong but to respect the weak as well, for the strengths and the weaknesses are, to a great extent, in us all. It is circumstance more than anything else which creates the one we would term weak or the one we would term strong.

This was another part of the reason why I so hated what the men of Cend-Amrid had become.

In the end, perhaps, it was to resolve itself into a matter of wits and sword-play. But you must know that my mind was at work before my sword-arm.

And if Mars is a preferable place to Earth you must understand why. The reason is this: Circumstances are kinder to Mars than Earth. There is little disease on the planet and the population is small enough to allow every man the chance of becoming himself.

The dead-faced man now opened a door and stood back to allow us to enter.

I was surprised to see another inhabitant of the small cell, which was fitted with four bunks. He was unlike the Eleven, but there was something about his haunted eyes that made me think of the physician we had first met.

"He not good for others here," said the dead-faced man, "but this only place for you. Not talk to him."

We said nothing as we entered the cell and watched the door close on us. We heard a bar drop and knew we were imprisoned. Only the fact that we still had our weapons comforted us.

"Who are you?" asked our cell-mate when the footfalls of the other man had died. "Why has Six imprisoned you and let you keep your swords?"

"He was Six, was he?" I smiled. "We were never introduced."

The man got up and came towards me angrily. "You laugh – at *that*?" He pointed towards the door. "Have you no understanding of what you are laughing at?"

I became serious. "Of course," I said, "but it seems to me that if action is to be taken against *that*" – I nodded in the direction he had pointed – "we must keep our heads and not become as mad, in our own way, as those we intend to fight."

He looked searchingly into my face and then cast his glance to the floor, nodding to himself.

"Perhaps you are right," he said. "Perhaps that is where I went wrong in the end."

I introduced my friend and myself. "This is Hool Haji, Prince of the Mendishar in the far North; and I am Michael Kane, Prince of Varnal, which lies to the South."

26

"Strange friends," he said, looking up. "I thought the folk of the South and the Blue Giants were hereditary enemies."

"Things aren't quite so bad now," I said. "But who are you and why are you here?"

"I am One," he said, "and I am here because of that, if you like."

"You mean you are the missing member of the council which rules Cend-Amrid?"

"Just so. More – I formed the council. Have you seen where they sit?"

"A bizarre place – yes."

"I put the skeleton in the centre of the table. It was meant to be a constant reminder of what we fought against – this horrible plague which still ravages the city."

"But what caused the plague? I have heard of no deadly disease on Mars."

"We caused it – indirectly. We found an ancient canister not far from the outskirts of the city. It was so old that it was obviously a creation of the Sheev or the Yaksha. It took us many months before we got it open."

"What was inside?" Hool Haji asked curiously.

"Nothing – we thought."

"Just air?" Hool Haji said, unbelievingly.

"Not just air – the plague. It had been there all the time. In our foolishness we released it."

Hool Haji nodded now. "Yes, I remember half a story," he said. "Something about how, in their war of self-destruction, the Sheev and the Yaksha used diseases which they somehow managed to trap and release on their enemies. That must be what you found."

"So we discovered – and at what cost!" The man who had called himself. One went and sat down on his bunk, his head in his hands.

"But what happened then?"

"I was a member of the council governing Cend-Amrid. I decided that in order to control the plague we must have a logical system. I decided – and, believe me, it was not a decision that I enjoyed reaching – that until the plague was wiped out we must regard every human being simply as a machine,

27

otherwise the plague would spread everywhere. If the plague did not affect the person very badly – and its effects vary, you know – then he could be considered a potentially functioning mechanism. If the plague affected him badly, then he was to be regarded as a useless mechanism, and thus to be destroyed, his useful parts to be stored in case they could contribute to a functioning, or potentially functioning, mechanism."

"But such a concept suggests that you have a much more sophisticated form of surgery than your society indicates," I said.

"We have the Sheev device. An arm, a hand, a vital organ may be inserted or attached where it should be in the human body, and then the Sheev machine is switched on. Some kind of force flows out of the machine – and knits the parts together." The man spoke wonderingly, as if I should have known this.

Hool Haji broke in. "I have heard of such a machine," he said, "but I had no idea that one existed in Cend-Amrid."

"We kept it a secret from other folk," said the man. "We are inclined to be a secretive people, as you might know."

"I knew that," Hool Haji agreed. "But I did not realize to what extent you guarded your secrets."

"Perhaps if we had not been so secretive," said One, "we should not be in this position today."

"It is hard to say," I told him. "But why are you now in prison?"

"Because I saw that my reasoning had produced something as dangerous as the plague," he replied. "I tried to reverse the course on which I had embarked, tried to steer us all back to sanity. It was too late."

I sympathized with him. "But they did not kill you. Why?"

"Because, I suppose, of my mind. In their own strange way they still respect intelligence – or, at least, intelligence of a certain kind. I don't think that will last."

Neither did I. I was moved to loathe and at the same time sympathize with the tragic man who sat on the bunk before me. But sympathy got the upper hand, though I privately cursed him for a fool. Like others before him, on Earth and

28

on Mars, he had become victim of the monster he had created.

"Did it not occur to you," I said, "that if the ancient people – the Sheev or the Yaksha – could devise this plague-canister, they might also have had another device that could cure the plague?"

"Naturally, it occurred to me," said One, looking up, offended. "But does it still exist? If so, where is it? How do you contact the Sheev?"

"No one knows," Hool Haji said. "They come and they go."

"Surely it must be possible," I said, looking at Hool Haji quickly, wondering if the same thought had struck him, "to discover this device – if it still exists."

Hool Haji looked up, his eyes lighting. "You are thinking of the place we were originally destined for, are you not?"

"I am," I said.

"Of course. Cure the plague – then cure the madness!"

"Exactly."

One was looking at us wonderingly, obviously utterly unaware of what we were talking about. I thought it expedient at this stage not to tell him of the treasure house of machines that lay hidden in the vaults of the Yaksha. Indeed, by mutual consent earlier, Hool Haji and I had agreed that the place should be secret and that only the minimum of trusted people should be told where it was. In this, we shared the apparent anxiety of the Sheev, feeling that there was a danger inherent in releasing such knowledge all at once. If the Sheev took the benevolent interest in humanity that I believed they did, then they were obviously waiting for the society on Mars to mature thoroughly before allowing them the benefits of the previous society which had destroyed itself.

One asked: "What are you saying? That there is a chance of finding a cure for the plague?"

"Just so."

"Where? And how?"

"We cannot say," I told him. "But if we manage to get away from Cend-Amrid, and if we do find such a machine, I assure you we shall be back."

"Very well," he said. "I accept this. You offer hope, at least, when I had thought all hope had gone."

"Tell us your real name," I said. "And restore a little hope in yourself."

"Barane Dasa," he said, rising again and speaking a little more levelly. "Barane Dasa, Master Smith of Cend-Amrid."

"Then wish us well and wish us luck, Barane Dasa," I said, "and hope that the Eleven will be able to help us repair our engine."

"We understand machines in Cend-Amrid," he said with something like a former pride coming into his eyes. "It will be repaired."

"Perhaps you did not understand them quite enough," I reminded him.

He pursed his lips. "Perhaps we did not make enough distinction between the machines we loved and the people we also loved," he said.

"It is a distinction we should always make," I told him. "But it does not mean we should reject the machines altogether. Distinctions are useful, rejections are not so useful, for the distinction comes from a love of knowledge while rejection of something comes from a fear of it, when all's said and done."

"I will think about that," he said, a faint smile touching his lips, "but I will think for some time before I decide whether or not to agree with you."

"It is all we should ask," I replied, returning his smile.

Then we went to sleep, Hool Haji stretching himself out on the floor of the cell, since the bunks were not designed for ten-foot high Blue Giants!

Chapter Four

FLIGHT FROM CEND-AMRID

IN the morning, soon after the sun had risen, we all went out to look at the engine – Hool Haji, myself, and the Eleven. I had learned from Barane Dasa that every member of the council had been at the top of his particular trade before the coming of the plague and understood that these were the best people to put the engine right if anyone could.

I brought the airship right down to the ground and stripped off the plates covering the engine housing. I could see almost immediately that the trouble was simple and swore at myself for a fool. The fuel pipe was in several sections and one of these had come loose. Somehow a piece of rag – perhaps overlooked by a mechanic – had worked its way into the pipe and was clogging it.

It is invariably the simple explanation that one ignores. I had assumed – quite fairly, since the mechanics I had trained in Varnal were normally very trustworthy and conscientious – that something was intrinsically wrong with the engine.

Still, I had found Cend-Amrid because of this mistake, and it was probably just as well, since I now had the chance to do something about it. It was not only the good of Cend-Amrid that I had at heart, but the good of the whole of Mars. I knew that both disease and creed could spread, in much the same way that the Black Death and Black Magic had been linked in the Middle Ages, and I wished to counter this at any cost.

I thought it expedient, however, to pretend that there was still something wrong with the engine and allowed the Eleven to inspect it, their faces as blank as ever, while I drew up the plans I had promised them. I was fairly certain that whatever fuel source they used, it would not be sufficiently sophisticated to allow them to get very far before I returned, since even steam-power was only understood by them in elementary terms. This, of course, made them very different from the rest

31

of the folk of Mars, who had never bothered themselves with physics, save the theoretical kind, since the Sheev machines were highly sophisticated and, to them, beyond understanding.

Once again I could sympathize with the folk of Cend-Amrid, but still felt that the situation existing throughout the rest of Mars to my knowledge was, in the end, for the best.

In short, curiosity only sometimes kills the cat, and then it usually happens because the cat hasn't found its feet properly.

I felt better for the knowledge that I could now leave Cend-Amrid without too much difficulty and watched for some sign of puzzlement on the faces of the Eleven as they studied my drawings.

There was none. The only impression I received from them was an impression of their confidence in themselves.

Inevitably, they came to ask me about the fuel and I showed them some of the gasolene which I had had refined in Varnal. I would point out that the Varnalians themselves did not really understand anything of the principles behind the engines I used for the airships, just as they did not understand the much more complicated principles behind the original Sheev engine I had used to power my first airship. This again, I felt, was at the moment for the best.

One of the Eleven – he called himself Nine – asked me about gasolene and where it could be found.

"It is not like this in its natural state," I told him.

"What is it like in natural state?" came the emotionless question.

"That is difficult to say."

"You come back Cend-Amrid and show. We have many liquids we keep from old discoveries."

Doubtless he meant that they had found other things left behind by the Sheev and preserved them in one way or another.

Now my curiosity got the better of me and I did not wish to miss the chance of seeing these "liquids" that Nine mentioned. I agreed to go back.

Leaving Hool Haji in the ship, I returned with the entire Eleven to their laboratory building which lay just behind the

32

Central Place. By daylight it was possible to see evidence of the plague everywhere. Carts creaked through the streets, loaded with corpses. But whereas one would have expected to see signs of grief on the faces of those who lived, there were few. The Eleven's tyranny did not allow such – to them – inefficient emotions as grief or joy. I gathered that signs of emotion were regarded either as indications of "insanity" or that the plague had infected another victim.

I shuddered more at this than I would have done had anyone shown a sign of grief.

The Eleven showed me all the chemicals they had discovered amongst the ruins of Sheev cities, but I told them that none was anything like gasolene – although I lied.

They asked me to leave a little gasolene with them, and I agreed. I intended to make sure, however, that it would not work when they tried it.

I had refused to be borne in one of their dreadful carriages, and so we walked back the way we had come.

This, although they did not show it, seemed distasteful to the Eleven and I realized exactly why when one of them paused. At the end of the street we were walking down I saw a man stagger from a house and come stumbling towards us.

There was bloody foam on his lips and his face had a greenish patch coming up from his neck to his nose. One arm seemed paralysed and useless, the other waved about as if he was trying to keep his balance. He saw us and an inarticulate cry came from his lips. His eyes were fever-bright and hatred shone from them.

As he drew close to the Eleven he shouted: "What have you done? What have you done?"

The Eleven turned as one man, leaving only myself to face the plague-stricken wretch.

But he ignored me and ran towards them.

"What have you done" he screeched again.

"Words mean nothing. Cannot answer," Nine replied.

"You are guilty! You released the plague. You imposed this wicked government upon us! Why will so few realize this?"

"Inefficient," came the cold, dead voice of Six.

Then, from the same doorway, a girl came running. She was pretty, about eighteen, and dressed in the normal Martian harness. Her brown hair was in disarray and her face was streaked with tears.

"Father!" she shouted, running towards the wretch.

"Go away, Ala Mara," he cried. "Go away – I am going to die. Let me use the little life left in me to protest to these tyrants. Let me try to make them feel something human – even if it's only hatred!"

"No, father!" The girl began to pull at his arm.

I spoke to her. "I sympathize with you both," I said. "But wait a little longer. I might be able to help."

One of the Eleven – I believe he called himself Three – turned. There was a dart-gun in his hand. Without even blinking, he pulled the trigger. The things only worked at short range – and this was almost point-blank. The man fell with a groan.

The girl gave a great shriek and began to hammer at Three's chest with her fists.

"You've killed him. You might at least have left him the little life he had!" she sobbed in rage.

"Inefficient," said Three. "You inefficient, too." He raised the gun.

I could stand no more.

With a wordless cry I leapt at him, knocking the gun from his hand and putting my arm around the girl.

I said nothing.

He said nothing.

We simply stood there regarding each other silently as the other ten members of the council turned.

With my free hand I drew my sword.

"A dead man is the most inefficient of all," I said. "And I can make several of you that if you move a step."

The girl was now weeping with reaction and my heart went out to her now even more than it had done before.

"Do not worry, Ala Mara," I said, remembering the name her dead father had used. "They will not harm you."

Now the furthest away from me put a whistle to his lips, ignoring my threat. Its note pierced the air and I knew that the whistle was intended to summon guards.

34

Heaving the girl on to my shoulder, I began to dash down the street. I knew that the gate was around the next bend and that if I could put enough distance between myself and the Eleven fast enough their dart-guns could not harm me.

I ran panting around the corner and rushed towards the open gate.

Guards were coming at me as I went through the gate and I prayed that I could reach the waiting airship before all was lost.

Hool Haji must have seen me being chased by the guards because he suddenly appeared at the entrance to the airship's cabin. I half flung the girl at him and turned just in time to engage the first couple of swordsmen.

They were inexpert with their weapons and I easily defended myself at first. But soon others joined the fight and I would have been hard pressed had not Hool Haji's massive bulk dropped down beside me.

Together we held them off until several lay dead or wounded on the ground.

Hool Haji muttered to me: "Get aboard. I'll join you at once."

Still fighting, I managed to clamber into the cabin.

Hool Haji made one last thrust, killing a guard and, in that split-second lull in the fighting, jumped into the cabin.

I was ready with the door and slammed it shut. Leaving Hool Haji to bolt it, I went past the still frightened girl and seated myself at my airship's controls.

It was only a matter of moments before the engine roared into powerful life. I released the anchor ropes and we were soon rising into the air.

"What now?" Hool Haji asked, glancing at the girl as he seated himself in his specially large chair.

"I am tempted to return at once to Varnal," I said, "and get the taste of that place out of my mouth before doing anything more. But it would probably be best to go at once to the Vaults of Yaksha and see if we can find a machine to cure the plague. Better yet – if we could contact the Sheev, they might help."

35

"The Sheev involve themselves rarely in our affairs," Hool Haji reminded me.

"But if they *knew*!"

"Perhaps they do."

"Very well," I said. "We go to Yaksha. Perhaps there we will also find a means of contacting the Sheev."

"What about the girl?" Hool Haji asked.

"There is nothing for it but to take her with us," I said, "after all, in helping her in the first place I have made her my responsibility."

"And mine, my friend." Hool Haji smiled, gripping my shoulder.

From behind us, Ala Mara said weakly: "I thank you, strangers. But if I am to be any trouble to you, put me down where you will. You have done enough."

"Nonsense," I said, setting course for the North and Yaksha. "I want to be able eventually to return you to Cend-Amrid – and when we do return it will be with some effective means of destroying both the tyrannies that dwell there."

Perhaps moved by this, and obviously remembering the death of her father, the girl began to sob again. I, too, found it hard to remain completely unaffected by her emotion and it was a long time before I could begin to work out what method I was going to use to find the machine that could cure the plague – assuming that it existed in Yaksha at all!

It would be several days yet before our destination would be reached. And in that time I would have to train myself to think very coolly indeed.

I did not know then, of course, just what was in store for me. If I had, I might have returned to Varnal.

As it was, things were to complicate themselves even more and I was going to find myself in desperate straits soon enough – as were we all!

Chapter Five

THE BARBARIANS

At last we were crossing the desert, having decided to visit
Mendishar, Hool Haji's homeland, on our way back. This was
partly my friend's decision, since he explained he had only
recently left there and was sure that there was little to concern him at present.

We dropped down just outside the entrance we had cleared
earlier. We secured the airship, leaving Ala Mara in charge of
it.

At the entrance, which had been covered with a great sheet
of non-corrosive metal alloy which we had found earlier, we
saw signs that it had been disturbed.

Hool Haji pointed at the ground.

"Men have been here since we last left," he said. "Here are
footmarks – and there signs that heavy objects have been dragged over the ground. What do you make of it, Michael Kane?"

I frowned. "No more than you at this stage. We had best
enter carefully. Perhaps inside we shall discover signs of the
identity of the strangers. Who would have been likely to come
here?"

Hool Haji shook his head. "The footprints show that they
were not folk of my race but of yours – and yet no small ones
dwell in these parts. They must have come from afar."

We lifted the covering and passed into the cool interior. It
was illuminated by the seemingly everlasting lights of the ancient race.

We had made wooden steps on our last visit, and these were
now chipped and battered, again indicating that heavy objects
had been dragged up them.

As we progressed further into the vaults of the Yaksha, we
gasped in anger at the destruction we saw. Machines had been
overturned and smashed, jars of chemicals had been spilt and
broken, artifacts of all kinds had been partially destroyed.

On we went, through the many chambers of the underground city, finding further evidence of insensate vandalism, until we stepped into a particularly large chamber and found it almost empty. I remembered that the place had contained many of the most interesting machines of the Yaksha, machines which would have produced much interesting knowledge when I got round to investigating them.

But they were gone!

Where were they?

I could not guess.

Just then my ears caught the sound of movement ahead of us and I drew my sword, Hool Haji following suit.

We had just done this when, from the opposite entrance to the one we had entered, a number of men came running, brandishing swords in their hands, round shields of crudely beaten metal on their arms.

The thing that struck me most about them, however, was the fact that they were all bearded. Almost everyone I had seen on Mars was clean-shaven.

These men were squat, muscular, with heavy leather harness completely unadorned. Their only decorations were necklaces and bangles of hammered metal, something like iron, though a few wore what appeared in that light to be gold or brass.

They came to a ragged halt as we prepared to meet them, our swords at the ready.

One of them, a squint-eyed individual even hairier than most of the others, cocked his head to one side and said in a harsh, insolent voice:

"Who are you? What are you doing here? These are our looting grounds. We found 'em first."

"Did you, indeed?" I replied.

"Yes, we did. You're a funny pair to be here together. I thought you Blue Giants were always fighting people like us."

"People like you need to be fought, judging by what you have done to this place," Hool Haji said in a tone of distaste.

"I mean people like *him*, too," said the bearded one, waving his sword in my direction.

38

"That is beside the point," I said impatiently. "What is more to the point is – who are *you*?"

"None of your business!"

"We can make it our business!" Hool Haji growled.

The bearded man laughed harshly and arrogantly. "Oh, can you? Well, you can try if you like. We're the Bagarad, and Rokin the Gold's our leader. We're the fiercest fighters on both sides of the Western Sea."

"So you come from over the Western Sea," I said.

"You've heard of us?"

I shook my head but Hool Haji said: "The Bagarad – I've heard a little of you from my father. Barbarians – looters – raiders from the land beyond the Western Sea."

I had only visited the Western continent once, and then by accident, when I had encountered the strange City of the Spider and Hool Haji and I had barely escaped with our lives. So these, too, were from that mysterious continent, unexplored by most civilized Martian nations.

"Barbarians!" Again the man voiced his guttural laugh. "Maybe – but we'll soon be conquerors of the world!"

"How so?" I asked, a suspicion dawning.

"Because we have weapons – weapons undreamed of by human beings. The weapons of the Gods who once dwelled here!"

"They were no Gods," I said. "Pitiful demons, perhaps."

The man frowned. "What do you know of the Gods?"

"I told you – those who built this city-vault were not Gods, they were simply men."

"You talk heresy, smoothskin," the barbarian growled. "Watch your step. Who are you, anyway?"

"I am Michael Kane, Bradhinak of Varnal."

"A Bradhinak, eh? Hmmm – could get good ransom for you, eh?"

"Doubtless," I said coldly. "But it would be ransom for a corpse, for I'd die fighting rather than have hands such as yours laid on me."

The barbarian grinned, enjoying the insult for its own sake.

"And who's the other?"

39

"I am Bradhi Hool Haji of Mendishar, and I need not repeat my friend's words, since they are the same as mine would be." Hool Haji shifted his stance slightly.

The barbarian lowered his squinting gaze thoughtfully.

"Well, well. Two good prizes if we can get you alive, aren't you? I'm Zonorn the Render – my name well-earned. I've torn men limb from limb in my time."

"A useful accomplishment," I said mockingly.

His face became serious. "Aye, it is – where the Bagarad rule. Nobody dare spit in Zonorn's eye – save the only man stronger than me."

"The way you speak, there isn't one," I said.

"I'm talking about our own Bradhi – Rokin the Gold. You can insult me and I'll judge the insult on its merits. Only if it's a weak one I'll complain. But say a word against Rokin – a true War Bradhi – and I'll tear you apart. I need no sword or shield when I deal with a man."

"So you, under Rokin's orders, have stolen the machines. Is that it?"

"That's it, roughly."

"Where are the machines now? Still on this side of the Western ocean?"

"Some are, some aren't."

"You are fools to tamper with them, you know. They could destroy you as easily as they could those you plan to use them against."

"Don't try to worry me with talk like that," Zonorn rasped. "We know what we're doing. Never call a man of the Bagarad a fool until you look for your beard." He burst into laughter, obviously enjoying what was a common jest amongst his people.

"I have no beard," I reminded him. "And you would be wise if you returned what you have stolen. You cannot understand the implications of what you have done, nor would you understand them if I explained them to you."

"We're not afraid of you," he muttered. "And we're not afraid of your big friend. There are a lot of us – and we're the best fighters any side of the ocean."

"Then we'll bargain," I said.

"What's the bargain?"

"If we beat you in fair fight, you bring back the weapons." I thought this would probably appeal to his simple barbarian instincts.

"Can't do that," he said, shaking his head as if disappointed. "Rokin would have to decide anything of that sort."

"Then what do we do?"

"I'm a fair man," Zonorn said thoughtfully. "And we're under strength at present. I'll let you go. How's that?"

"You're afraid to fight us, is that it?" Hool Haji laughed, hefting his sword.

It was the wrong thing to have said.

If Zonorn had let us go we could have returned with a force of Mendishar to stop them before they embarked in their ships for the Western continent.

But Hool Haji had attacked Zonorn's barbarian pride.

It could only be settled in blood now.

With a roar of anger, Zonorn was already rushing at Hool Haji.

His men came at us, too.

Soon the pair of us were fighting several whirling blades apiece. The barbarians were hardy, powerful fighters, but lacked finesse in their sword-play.

It was fairly easy to defend ourselves, even against so many, but we both knew we should be killed very soon unless we were remarkably lucky.

Our backs were against the wall as we fought, and our blades were soon stained from tip to hilt with the blood of our attackers.

I dodged a clumsy thrust and stabbed over a shield-rim, taking my assailant in the throat. It was only when I had killed him and was already engaged with another opponent, that I realized I had killed Zonorn himself.

After a time my sword-arm began to ache, but I fought on desperately, knowing that there was much more at stake in this fight than our own lives.

The fate of Cend-Amrid was in the balance. Perhaps even the fate of the whole of Mars.

We had to find the right machine, either in the vaults or in the possession of the untutored barbarian who called himself Rokin the Gold.

I blocked a blow from above and was half winded when my attacker shoved at my chest with his shield.

I slid my sword down to his hilt, suddenly disengaged and then thrust forward again, contriving to take him in the heart.

Yet it seemed that as fast as we killed them there were others to take their places and, as usual, I soon lost all thought of anything but the fight. I became, for all that I loathed it, a fighting machine myself, my whole attention focused on preserving my life, even though it meant taking so many other lives in the process.

For all my fine ideas, when it came down to it I was as much a killer as others I despised for that reason.

I say this only to show that I do not enjoy killing and avoid it where I can, even on Mars – that warlike world.

On and on we fought, until all sense of time was lost and it seemed, over and over again, that we escaped death by a hair's breadth.

But it seemed at last that our assailants were tiring, too. I saw a break and decided that, in this case, we would serve our purpose best if we tried to escape.

With a roar to Hool Haji, I dived through the gap, seeing from the corner of my eye that he was following me.

Then, from somewhere in the shadows, I saw another man dart at Hool Haji's side. I knew instinctively that Hool Haji would not see him in time.

With a yell of warning I turned to save him. I turned too sharply and lost my footing in slippery blood.

I remember a grinning, bearded face and a shield smashing forward into my own.

I tried to keep a grip on my senses, struggled to rise. I saw Hool Haji clutch at his side, grimacing with pain. Then my vision clouded.

I fell forward, certain that I would never wake again.

Chapter Six

ROKIN THE GOLD

I DID wake again, but it was not a comfortable awakening. I was being jolted along on the back of an animal.

Opening my eyes, blinking in the glare of harsh sunlight, I saw that I was tied hand and foot, strapped over the back of a large dahara, the universal riding animal and pack beast of all the Martians I had ever encountered.

The sun was shining directly in my eyes, I had a headache and every muscle in my body ached. But I seemed generally in one piece.

I wondered what had become of Hool Haji.

And then I wondered what had happened to Ala Mara, whom we had left in charge of the airship.

I prayed that the coarse barbarians had not discovered her!

I closed my eyes against the sunlight, beginning to think of ways of escaping from my captors, ways of finding the machine – if it existed – for curing the plague in Cend-Amrid. I was so tired that it was difficult to think logically.

The next time I opened my eyes I was staring into the leering face of a barbarian.

"So you live." He grinned. "I thought you southern folk weak – but we learned otherwise back there."

"Give me a sword and untie my hands and you'll learn that lesson personally," I said thickly.

He shook his head wonderingly. "Give you a beard and you could be a Bagarad. I think Rokin the Gold will like you."

"Where are we going?"

"To see Rokin."

"What happened to my friend?" I deliberately did not mention the girl.

"He lives, too – though he got a slight flesh wound." We were still moving as he spoke – he was riding a dahara. I was filled with relief that Hool Haji had survived.

43

"We could not find your daharas," said the barbarian. "How did you get here?"

I was further relieved on hearing this question, because it meant they had not discovered Ala Mara. But where was she? Why had they not noticed the airship? I tried to reply in a way that would answer these questions for me, at least partially.

"We had an air vessel," I said. "We flew here."

The barbarian guffawed.

"You've got guts," he said. "You can lie like a Bagarad as well as fight like one."

"You saw no airship?"

He grinned. "We saw no airship. You call us barbarians, my friend, but even we know enough not to believe in children's stories. Everyone knows that men aren't meant to fly – and can't, therefore."

I smiled weakly back. He did not know that I smiled at his naïveté and because this certainly meant they had not seen either my airship or Ala Mara. But I still wondered what had happened to the girl.

Perhaps the airship had somehow drifted away. I could not guess. I could only hope that both were safe.

After a while my exhaustion caused me to fall asleep in spite of the rough ride I was having.

When next I awoke it was dark and the dahara was moving at a slower pace.

Above the murmur of the barbarians' conversation I heard another murmur – the murmur of the sea.

With a sinking heart I realized that we had come to the barbarians' base and I was soon to face their much-admired leader, Rokin the Gold.

The dahara stopped after a while and heavy hands hauled the straps away from my body and dumped me on the ground. One of the barbarians, perhaps the one I had spoken to earlier, put a skin of tepid water to my lips and I drank thirstily.

"Food soon," he promised. "After you've been looked over by Rokin."

He went away and I lay on hard shingle, listening to the nearby sounds of the sea. I was still half in a daze.

Later I heard voices and there was a thump. I turned my head and saw the great bulk of Hool Haji lying beside me. I noticed his wound and saw that at least the barbarians had had the grace to dress it, though crudely.

He turned his head and smiled at me grimly.

"At least we live," he said.

"But for how long?" I said. "And will it be worth it? We must escape as soon as possible, Hool Haji. You know why!"

"I know," he said evenly. "Thoughts of escape are well in my mind. But at present we can only bide our time. What of the girl you rescued from Cend-Amrid – where is she?"

"Safe, as far as I know," I told him. "Or, at least, she was not captured by the barbarians."

"Good. How did you discover this?"

I told him the little I had learned.

"Perhaps she saw something of what happened and went for help," he said, though clearly not convinced.

"She could not operate the controls unless she had watched me very carefully indeed. I can think of no explanation. I just hope that she will be all right."

"Have you noticed one thing?" Hool Haji asked then. "The one real chance we have?"

"What's that?"

"The secret skinning knife is still in my harness."

That was something! All blue Martians carry small knives hidden in their ornate war harness. To someone not used to looking for such things, it seemed part of the general decoration of the harness, but I had had cause to thank those secret knives once before. Unfortunately, I now wore a Southern-style harness that did not contain a knife. Still, one was better than none. If I could reach it with my teeth, I might be able to cut Hool Haji's bonds.

I was rolling towards him with this intention when suddenly there came a sound from above. I rolled back and looked up.

Framed against the sky, which was lit only by Phobos, I saw a gigantic figure, clad all in bright metal. The metal was gold, crudely fashioned into armour, with great, bent rivets plainly visible, holding it all together. It was a splendid picture of barbarian grandiose ostentation, and the man wore it well enough.

He had a finely combed yellow beard and hair to match, long and flowing and plainly cleaner than that of his fellows. At his hip he wore a huge broadsword, the hilt of which he gripped as he looked down at me, a vast grin spreading across his face.

"Which are you," he said in a deep, humorous voice, "the Bradhi or the Bradhinak?"

"Which are *you*?" I said, though I guessed the obvious.

"Bradhi, my friend, as you well know if you've talked as much to my men as they say. Bradhi Rokin the Gold, leader of these hounds, the Bagarad. Now – be civil and answer me."

"I am the Bradhinak Michael Kane of Varnal, City of the Green Mists, most beautiful in the whole of Vashu." I spoke as grandiosely, using the Martian word for their planet.

He grinned again. "And you – the other one. You must be the Bradhi, then, eh?"

"Bradhi of a long line," Hool Haji said proudly. "Bradhi of the Mendishar – there is no greater boast."

"You think not, eh?"

Hool Haji did not reply. He looked at Rokin with an unwinking stare.

Rokin did not seem to mind.

"You killed a lot of my men, I'm told, including my finest lieutenant, Zonorn the Render. I thought him unkillable."

"It was easy," I said. "It was incidental. I did not realize he was one of those I killed until after I had done it."

Rokin roared with laughter. "What a boaster! Better than a Bagarad!"

"Some, I've been told," I said. "It is not difficult to believe if they are all like Zonorn."

He frowned a little, though he still grinned, pointing at me, his golden armour creaking at the joints. "You think so? You'll find there are few to beat the Bagarad."

"Few what?"

"Eh? What d'you mean?"

"Few what? Children?"

"No! Men, my friend!" His face cleared. Like many primi-

46

tive people he seemed to appreciate an insult for its own sake, whether levelled at him or not. I knew, however, that there was a point that could be over-stepped and it was not always easy to see it. I did not bother to worry about it.

"What are you going to do with us now?" I asked him.

"I'm not sure. They say you seemed concerned about the weapons I've removed from that place we found. What do you know about them?"

"Nothing," I said.

"They say you seemed to know a great deal about them."

"Then they were wrong."

"Tell him to give them back," growled Hool Haji. "Tell him what we told his friend – they're fools to meddle with such power!"

"So you do know something." Rokin mused. "How much?"

"We only know that to tamper with them will mean death for you all, at the very least. It could mean the destruction of half of Mars!"

"Do not try to frighten me with such threats," Rokin smiled. "I am no little boy to be told what is bad for me and what is good."

"In this case," I said urgently, "you are as the smallest child. And these are no toys you are playing with!"

"I know that, my friend. They are weapons. Weapons that will win me half Mars if I use them well."

"Forget about them!" I said.

"Nonsense. Why should I?"

"For one thing," I told him, "there is a plague in a city some distance from here. One of the machines you have might be capable of checking it. If it is not checked it must soon escape the confines of the city and begin to spread. Do you know what a plague is? A disease?"

"Well, I've had one or two complaints myself – so have others I know. I was coughing for a couple of days when I lost myself swimming in the ocean when I was a lad. Is that what you mean?"

"No." I described the symptoms of the green plague that was destroying the folk of Cend-Amrid.

47

He looked rather green himself when I had finished. "Are you sure it's that bad?" he said.

"It is," I said. "What would you think if something like that swept throughout this continent, eventually spreading to your own?"

"How can it 'spread'?" he said unbelievingly.

I tried to explain about germs and microbes, but it meant nothing to him. All I succeeded in doing was weakening my case and leaving him shaking his head.

"What a liar! What a liar!" he repeated. "Little creatures in our blood! Ho! Ho! Ho! You must be a Bagarad. You must have been stolen from us as a baby!"

"Believe what I tell you about the plague or not," I said desperately. "But believe its effects, at least – even Rokin the Gold is not safe from it."

He tapped his armour. "This is gold – it protects me from anything – man or magic!"

"You seem to respect us," I said. "Then will you release us?"

He shook his head. "No." He grinned. "I think we'll find you useful – if only for ransom."

It was impossible, plainly, to reach the barbarian by appealing to his reason. There was nothing for it but to hope we could make an early escape, after seeing just what machines he had stolen and, if possible, making sure he could never use them. This gave rise to another thought.

"What if I can help with the machines?" I said. "Would you release us then?"

"Perhaps," he said, nodding thoughtfully. "If I decided to trust you."

"I am a scientist," I informed him. "I might throw in my lot with you if you made it worth my while."

This line of attack seemed to be getting better results, for he rubbed his jaw and nodded again.

"I'll think about all this," he said, "and talk to you again in the morning." He turned and began to stride down the beach. "I'll have some food sent to you," he called, as an afterthought.

The food was brought and it was not bad – honest, plain

meat, herbs and vegetables. It was fed to us by two grinning barbarians whose weak jokes we were forced to put up with as we ate.

When they had gone and the barbarian camp seemed still, I again began to roll towards Hool Haji, intent on getting at the knife in his harness.

Being tied so firmly, it was hard to tell if anyone could see us or not. I decided to take the chance.

Inch by inch I got closer to my friend, and at last my teeth were in the pommel of the secret knife.

Slowly I worked it out of its hiding place until it was firmly clamped in my teeth.

Hool Haji's hands were tied behind his back, so that now he had to roll over while I tried to saw at his bonds.

After what seemed an age the first strand parted, then the second. Very soon his hands would be free!

I was just starting on the last piece of rope securing Hool Haji's hands when there came a gruff laugh from above and I glimpsed gold as the knife was snatched from my teeth.

"You're game, the pair of you," came Rokin's voice, full of rough laughter. "But you're too valuable to let go. We'd better send you to sleep again."

Hool Haji and I made a desperate attempt to get to our feet and attack him, but our bonds had checked our circulation.

A sword-pommel was raised.

It descended.

I blacked out.

Chapter Seven

VOYAGE TO BAGARAD

WE were at sea when I awoke in the musty-smelling hold of a ship whose sides did not seem to be of wood, as I had expected.

My bonds had been cut, and apart from slight cramp in my muscles I was feeling much better physically. I was also thinking with greater clarity. The recent experiences with the barbarians seemed to have drained me of much of my original emotion and, while I knew it would return in time, I felt detached and, in some ways, in a healthier state of mind. Perhaps it was the ship. The space is confined, the possibilities limited, and thus one feels more in control of one's environment, particularly in contrast to the seemingly limitless horizons existing on Mars of the age I know.

Whatever the reasons – and they were probably an amalgam of all those I have suggested and more – I could work out better what I must do. The first objective must be to inspect all the machines Rokin had looted and check if one of them had properties capable of acting against the plague. If one should prove to have this property then I should have to think of ways of getting it away from Rokin and – the thought appalled me, but it was going to be necessary – destroy the rest. If none of the machines could provide me with what I wanted, then I could destroy them all. The latter would be the easier task, of course.

The ship was rolling and I was forced to brace myself against the sides of the hold. The hull seemed made in one piece, of a kind of durable plastic that I had discovered earlier in the Yaksha stronghold. It was dark, but as my eyes became accustomed to it, I could make out objects that might once have been engine mountings. But there were no engines now. Here again was an artifact left over from what the Martians call the Mightiest War – the war that almost totally eliminated both the Yaksha and the Sheev and virtually destroyed the planet itself.

I heard a stifled groan from the opposite corner. I thought I recognized the voice.

"Hool Haji?" I said. "Is it you?"

"It is I, my friend – or what is left of me. One moment while I make sure I am all in one piece. Where are we?"

Through the dimness I saw my comrade's huge shape rise from where he had been lying, saw him stagger and fall against a bulwark.

As best I could, I made my way towards him as the ship pitched about dreadfully. Though little sound permeated the hold, I had the impression that we were in the middle of a particularly unpleasant storm. I had heard that the Western ocean was not thought a healthy place for seafarers, which was probably why it was so infrequently crossed.

Hool Haji groaned. "Oh, the Mendishar were never meant to travel on the sea, Michael Kane."

He shifted his position as the ship was struck by another great wave.

Suddenly light streamed into the hold and sea water rushed in with it, soaking us at once. Framed in the opening above was a bearded barbarian.

"On deck!" he ordered curtly, his voice just heard above the howl of the storm.

"In this!" I said. "We're not seamen!"

"Then this is the time to become seamen, my friend. Rokin wants to see you."

I shrugged and made my way to the ladder now revealed in the light of the open hatch.

Hool Haji followed me.

Together we climbed out on to the slippery deck, clinging to the rope that ran along the centre of the deck, looped between the two large masts, their sails now reefed.

Spray swirled in the air, water slapped the deck, the ship was tumbled about by the great grey mass of heaving water. Sky and sea were grey and indistinguishable – everything seemed to be moving below us and about us. I had never experienced such a dreadful storm.

51

If a Blue Giant can turn green, then Hool Haji's face was green, his eyes showing a kind of agony that seemed to come as much from a deep-rooted disturbance in his soul as much as from the physical discomfort.

We edged our way towards the bridge of the ship, where Rokin, still in his golden armour, clung to the rail, looking about him as if in wonderment.

Somehow we managed to join him on the bridge.

He turned to us, saying something I could not catch in a tone that matched the wonderment in his gaze. I indicated that I had not heard him.

"Never seen one like this!" he shouted. "We'll be lucky if we stay up."

"What did you want to see us for?" I asked.

"Help!" he shouted.

"What can we do? We know nothing of ships or seafaring."

"There are machines in the hold, forward. They're powerful. Couldn't they calm the storm?"

"I doubt it," I yelled back.

He nodded to himself, then looked into my face. He appeared to accept the truth of what I said.

"What are our chances?" I asked.

"Poor!"

He still seemed to show little fear. He was, perhaps, more incredulous at the intensity of the storm.

Just then another great wave struck the ship and water came crashing down upon me. Then I felt Rokin's weighted bulk fall on me.

I heard a cry.

Then I knew that I had been hurled off the ship and was totally at the mercy of the raging ocean.

I struggled desperately to stay afloat, keeping mouth and nostrils as closed as possible.

I was hurtled crazily upon the crests of waves, crashing into valleys with walls of water, until I saw a trailing rope. I did not know if it was attached to anything or not – but I grabbed and caught it. I clung to the rope and felt the comfort of resistance at the other end.

I do not know for how long I clung to the rope, but whatever it was attached to the other end kept me afloat until the storm slowly abated.

I opened salt-encrusted eyes in the watery light of an early sunrise.

I saw a mast floating in the water ahead of me. My rope was fastened to it.

I hauled myself towards the broken mast, dragging myself wearily through the water. Then, as I neared it, I could see that several others were clinging to the mast.

When at length I grasped the mast, with a feeling of relief out of all proportion to the safety the mast offered, I saw that one of those who clung there, barely conscious, was Hool Haji, his great head lolling with exhaustion.

I reached out to touch him, to give him comfort and to let him know I still lived.

At that moment I heard a distant cry to my left and, looking in that direct, saw that the hull of the ship was miraculously still afloat.

Sunlight flashed on gold and I knew that Rokin had also survived. Clamping the rope between my teeth, I struck out towards the ship. At length the rope ran out before I had reached the ship but, luckily, it was drifting in my direction.

Soon I was being dragged on board and some of the barbarians were hauling in the rope and the mast.

It was not long before Hool Haji was also being helped aboard and we lay together, utterly weary, on the deck. Rokin, seemingly just as weary, was leaning on a broken rail and looking down on us.

From somewhere a hot drink was brought to us and we felt recovered enough to sit up and view the ship.

Virtually everything had been stripped from the deck by the fury of the storm. Only the miraculous hull had survived, relatively undamaged. Both masts had been ripped away, and most of the rails and all the deck furniture, including one of the hatch-covers, had been swept overboard.

Rokin walked towards us.

"You were lucky," he said.

"And you," I replied. "Where are we?"

"Somewhere on the Western sea. Perhaps, judging by the

direction of the storm, closer to our own land than yours. We can only hope that the currents are in our favour and that we shall soon reach land. Most of our provisions were ruined when yonder hold filled." He pointed to the hold that had had its cover ripped off. "The machines are down there, too – also half immersed – but safe enough, I'd guess."

"They will never be safe – to you," I warned him.

He grinned. "Nothing can harm Rokin – not even that storm."

"If I am right about the power of those machines," I told him, "they threaten far more danger than the storm."

"To Rokin's enemies, perhaps," retaliated the barbarian.

"To Rokin, too."

"What harm can they do to me? I have them."

"I have warned you," I said, shaking my head.

"What do you warn me about?"

"Your own ignorance!" I said.

He shrugged. "One does not have to be so full of knowledge to use such machines."

"Certainly," I agreed. "But one needs knowledge to understand them. If you do not understand them, then you will fear them soon enough."

"I do not follow your reasoning, Bradhinak. You are boring me."

Once again I gave up trying to argue with the barbarian, though I knew that in this case, as in all things, it is not enough to know that something works. One must also understand how it works before it can be used to advantage, and used without personal danger.

Chapter Eight

THE CRYSTAL PIT

THE ship reached land the next day – whether the mainland of the Western continent or an island I did not then know.

We leaped from the ship into the shallows, plunging thankfully up to the firm shore, while Rokin directed his men to beach the hull.

When this was done and we sat in the shadow of the hull, recovering from what we had endured in the past two days, Rokin turned to me with a faint trace of his old grin.

"So now we are all far from home – and far from our glory," he said.

"Thanks to you," said Hool Haji, echoing my own sentiments.

"Well," said Rokin, fingering his golden beard, now clogged with salt, "I suppose it is."

"Have you no idea where we are?" I asked him.

"None."

"Then we had best strike off along the coast in the hope of finding a friendly settlement," I suggested.

"I suppose so." He nodded. "But someone must stay to guard the treasures still in the ship."

"You mean the machines?" Hool Haji said.

"The machines," Rokin agreed.

"We could guard them," I said, "with the aid of some of your men."

Rokin laughed aloud. "Barbarian I may be, my friend, but fool I am not. No, you come with us. I'll leave some of my men to guard the ship."

And so we set off along the shore. It was a wide, smooth beach, with an occasional rock standing out from the sand and, far away, its foliage waving gently in the mild, warm breeze, was semi-tropical forest.

It seemed a peaceful enough place.

But I was wrong.

By mid-afternoon the shore had narrowed and we were walking much closer to the forest than before. The sky was overcast and the air had become colder. Hool Haji and myself had no cloaks and we shivered slightly in the still, chill air.

When they came, they came suddenly.

They came in a howling pack, bursting from the trees and running down the beach towards us. Grotesque parodies of human beings, waving clubs and crudely-hammered swords, covered in hair and completely naked.

I could not at first believe my eyes as I drew my own sword without thinking and prepared to face them.

Though they walked upright, they had the half-human faces of dogs – bloodhounds were the nearest species I could think of.

What was more, the noises they made were indistinguishable from the baying of hounds.

So bizarre was their appearance, so sudden their assault, that I was almost off my guard when the first club-brandishing dog-man came in to the attack.

I blocked the blow with my blade and sheered off the creature's fingers, finishing him cleanly with a thrust at his heart.

Another took his place, and more besides. I saw that we were completely surrounded by the pack. Apart from Hool Haji, Rokin and myself, there were only two other barbarians in our party and there were probably some fifty of the dog-men.

I swung my sword in an arc and it bit deep into the necks of two of the dog-men, causing them to fall.

The hounds' faces were slobbering and the large eyes held a maniacal hatred which I had only previously seen in the eyes of mad dogs. I had the impression that if they bit me I would be infected with rabies.

Three more fell before my blade as all the old teaching of M. Clarchet, my French fencing master since childhood, came back to me.

Once again I became cool.

Once again I became nothing more than a fighting machine, concentrating entirely on defending myself against this mad attack.

We held them off far longer than I had expected we could, until the press became so intense I could no longer move my sword.

The fighting then became a thing of fists and feet, and I went down with at least a dozen of the dog-men on top of me.

I felt my arms grasped, and still I tried to fight them off. But at length they had bound me.

Once again I had become a prisoner.

Would I survive to save Cend-Amrid?

I had now begun to doubt it. Ill-luck was riding me, I was sure, and I felt that I would meet my death on that mysterious Western continent.

The dog-men carried us into the forest, conversing in a sharp, barking form of the common Martian tongue. I found it hard to understand them.

Once I glimpsed Hool Haji being carried along by several of the dog-men, and I also saw a flash of Rokin's golden armour, so I assumed he lived, too. But I never saw the remaining barbarians again, so I concluded they had been slain.

Eventually the forest opened out on to a clearing and there was a village. The houses were only roughly-made shelters, but they had been built on, or among, the shells of far older stone buildings that did not seem to have any associations with either the Sheev or the Yaksha. The buildings must once have been massive and durable, but they had been erected by a more primitive race than the ancient race which had destroyed itself in the Mightiest War.

As we were carted into one of the shelters and dumped on the evil-smelling floor – half of stone, half of hardened mud – I wondered about the race that had abandoned the settlement before the dog-people had discovered it.

Before I could say anything to Hool Haji or Rokin about this, a dog-man, larger than the rest, entered the shelter and looked down at us out of his large, canine eyes.

"Who are you?" he said in his strange accent.

"Travellers," I replied. "We offer you no harm. Why did you attack us?"

"For the First Masters," he replied.

"Who are the First Masters?" asked Hool Haji from where he lay beside me.

"The First Masters are they who feed from the Crystal Pit."

"We do not know them," I said. "Why did they tell you to attack us?"

"They did not tell us."

"Do they give you your orders?" Rokin said. "If so, tell them they have made a prisoner of Rokin the Gold and his men will punish them if Rokin dies."

Something like a smile touched the heavy mouth of the dog-man.

"The First Masters punish – *they* are not punished."

"Can we speak to them?" I asked.

"They do not speak."

"Can we see them?" Hool Haji asked.

"You will see them – and they will see you."

"Well, at least we might be able to reason with these First Masters," I said to Hool Haji. I returned my attention to the dog-man who seemed to be the leader of the pack.

"Are these First Masters like you?" I asked. "Or are they like us?"

The pack-leader shrugged. "Like neither," he said. "Like that one more." And he pointed to Hool Haji.

"They are folk of my race?" Hool Haji said, brightening a little. "Then surely they can see that we wish them no harm."

"Only like you," said the dog-man. "Not the same as you. You will see them in the Crystal Pit."

"What is this Crystal Pit?" Rokin growled. "Why can't we see them now?"

Again the dog-man seemed to smile. "They do not come yet," he replied.

"When will they come?"

"Tomorrow – when the sun is hightest."

With that the dog-man left the shelter.

Somehow we managed to get some sleep, hoping that the mysterious First Masters would be more forthcoming and more open to reason than the dog-men, who were apparently their servants in some capacity we could not understand.

Just before noon on the next day several dog-men entered the shelter and picked us up, hauling us from the place and out into the daylight.

The pack-leader was waiting, standing on a piece of fallen masonry, a sword in one hand and a stick in the other. At the tip of the stick gleamed a ruby-like gem of incredible size. I did not understand its significance, save that perhaps it was some sign of the dog-man's leadership over the rest.

We were borne out of the clearing and into the forest again, but it was not long before the forest gave way to another and much larger clearing, with the farther trees a great distance away. Here lush grass waved, rising waist high and brushing my face as they carried me.

The grass soon became sparser, revealing an area of hardened mud in the centre of which was a great expanse of some gleaming substance which made my eyes ache.

It scintillated, flashing in the sun like a vast diamond.

It was only as we came closer that I realized that this must be the Crystal Pit.

It was a pit. Its sides were formed of pure, faceted crystal that caught the light from so many angles that it was almost impossible to guess what it was at first.

But where were these First Masters who looked like Hool Haji? I saw no one but my companions and the dog-men who had brought us here.

We were carried to the edge of the blinding pit and our bonds were cut. We looked about wondering what was to happen and none of us was prepared for the sudden shoves we received. Luckily the pit's sides were not particularly steep. We slid down to the bottom, barely able to check our descent, and landed in a heap at the bottom of the Crystal Pit.

As we picked ourselves up we saw the dog-men retreating from the edge of the pit.

We were unable to guess why we were there, but we were

all of us uneasy, suspecting that we were not merely to be imprisoned in the Crystal Pit indefinitely.

After about an hour, during which we were forced to keep our eyes closed most of the time, we gave up trying to scramble up the sides of the pit and began to try to work out some other means of escaping.

There seemed none.

Then we heard a sound from above and saw a face peering down at us.

At first we thought this must be one of the First Masters, but the face did not fit their description.

Then we saw that it was the face of a girl.

But perhaps girl is the wrong word, for the face, though intelligent and pleasant to look at, was the mutated face of a cat. Only the eyes and the pointed ears were evidence of the girl's non-simian ancestry, but it was as much a surprise to see this cat-girl as it had been to see the dog-men earlier.

"Are you enemies of the Hounds of Hahg?" came the whispered enquiry from the cat-girl.

"It seems that they think of us as such," I replied. "Are you, too, their enemy?"

"All my people – and they are few these days – hate the dog-folk of Hahg," she replied vehemently. "Many have been brought here to meet the First Masters."

"Are they your masters, too?" Hool Haji asked.

"They were – but we rejected them."

"Have you come to save us, girl?" came Rokin's voice, practical and impatient.

"I have come to try, but there is little time. Here." She reached over the edge of the pit and slid some objects down the sides. I saw at once that they were three swords, unlike those we had seen used by the dog-folk, but still strange. They were shorter than the swords I was used to, but of excellent workmanship. Picking one up and handing the others to my companions, I inspected it.

It was light and beautifully tempered. A little too light for my taste, but far better than nothing. I felt a little better.

I looked up and saw that the cat-girl's face had suddenly become anxious.

"Too late to help you from the pit," she said. "The First Masters come. I wish you well."

And then she was gone.

We waited tensely, swords in hand, wondering from where the First Masters would appear.

Chapter Nine

THE FIRST MASTERS

THEY came from above, their vast wings flapping noisily in the still air.

They were somewhat smaller than Hool Haji, but very like him in basic appearance, though their skins were of a much paler blue, a strange, unhealthy blue that contrasted oddly with their red, gaping mouths and their long, white tusks. Their wings spread partially from their shoulders, partially from around their hips.

They seemed more like beasts than men.

Perhaps, as the beasts had become men in the shape of the dog-folk and the cat-girl who had given us our swords, these men had become beasts. There was a strange, insensate glow in their eyes that did not seem to reflect the madness of men but the madness of the beast.

They hovered above us, their huge wings beating the air, causing a stiff wind to ruffle our hair.

"The Jihadoo!" Hool Haji gasped unbelievingly.

"What are they?" I asked, my gaze fixed on the weird creatures above.

"They are legends in Mendishar – an ancient race, similar to my own folk, who were shunned from our lands because of their dark, magical experiments."

"Magic? I thought no one in Mendishar believed in such stuff!" I said.

"Of course not. I told you, the Jihadoo were simply a legend. But now I am no longer certain of anything."

"Whatever you call them, they mean us ill," Rokin the Gold growled, blinking his eyes against the glare of the Crystal Pit.

One by one the First Masters – or the Jihadoo, as Hool Haji called them – began to cluster downwards into the pit.

Horrified, I prepared to defend myself.

The first one came sweeping down uttering a shrill scream,

red mouth gaping, fangs bared, claw-fingered hands extended to clutch me.

I slashed at the hand and drew blood. At least the Jihadoo were mortal, I remembered thinking as it swerved in the air and attacked me from another direction. Now others had joined the first and my comrades were as beset as myself.

I stabbed with the slim sword at the face of my first attacker and had the satisfaction of taking him in the eye and killing him.

The First Masters were plainly unprepared for armed resistance and this was why we survived the first encounters with comparative ease.

Another came at me, exposing his chest for a perfect stab into his chest.

The fairly narrow base of the pit helped us, since not too many of the Jihadoo could get at us at one time, but now we were forced to clamber on to the corpses of those we had already slain. In some ways this gave us a firmer footing as we fought.

All was a confusion of beating wings and fanged faces, glaring eyes and clutching claw-hands. I lopped another's head off, recoiling as sticky, evil-smelling blood spurted at my face.

Then, suddenly, as I engaged yet another of the monsters, I felt my shoulders seized in a painful grip.

I tried to turn, to slash at my attacker, but even as I did so I was hauled into the air and lost my balance for a moment.

I was being borne upwards into the air by one of the flying man-beasts.

High above the forest now, I still tried to destroy my captor, even if it meant my own destruction, so abhorrent did it seem to me.

I saw that Hool Haji and Rokin were in a similar plight to my own, but the few First Masters who followed us made me realize with a grim satisfaction just how many of their fellows we had killed.

Twisting in the painful grasp of the claws half-embedded in my shoulders, I tried to stab backwards at the arms or the torso.

To my right I saw Rokin attempt the same thing and, because of his golden armour, manage to twist one shoulder out of the Jihadoo's clutches.

Hanging by the arm which the Jihadoo still clasped, he began to slash at the centre's chest.

The creature did not retaliate, as I had expected. It simply released its grip on Rokin's other arm.

In horror I saw the barbarian yell and began to hurtle towards the rocky ground that had given way to the forest.

I saw his golden armour twisting in the sunlight, falling rapidly earthwards.

Then I saw it strike the ground.

I saw the armour split open on impact and a red corpse roll for a moment before becoming still.

I was sickened by the sight.

I knew that Rokin had been a barbarian and an enemy, but he had been a warm-blooded and, in his own way, generous man – a human being in the full sense.

And, with Rokin gone, we might never discover the rest of the machines he had stolen from the Yaksha – assuming, of course, the unlikely event of our surviving our present predicament.

I swung myself back now, curling my legs around one of the trailing legs of the Jihadoo. He did not seem to have anticipated this. Neither had I. It had been sudden inspiration, and now I at least had some chance of clinging on if he decided to release his grip.

Next, I managed to shift my position so that I was able to stab at his side with my sword. I began jabbing.

The wounds I was able to inflict were not serious, but they were sufficient to set him screaming and hissing.

I felt his grip begin to weaken and readied myself for what must happen next.

I stabbed several more times.

He screamed even more loudly. One claw released my shoulder and I ducked as he began to flail at me with it. I slashed at the clawed hand – and severed it.

This was too much for him. He dropped his remaining grip and I fell forward.

64

Only my legs, twisted around one of his, prevented me from joining Rokin.

I hurled my body through the air and managed to get another grip on his leg, this time with one of my arms.

He shook the leg, losing his equilibrium in the air and slowly beginning to descend, in spite of himself, as his wings beat to keep him up.

Bit by bit, and to my intense satisfaction, we began to go lower and lower as he struggled now to free himself. But I still clung to him, stabbing with the light sword.

He was bleeding profusely and getting weaker all the time.

Then, suddenly, with one final convulsion, he managed to loosen my grip.

With a feeling that all had been for nothing, I lost my hold and began to fall.

I did not fall for long, luckily, for once again the rocky ground had been replaced by forest and I fell into the branches of a tree. The supple bows held me like a soft hammock and after a moment I was able to climb out and begin to clamber to the ground.

I was worried about Hool Haji.

How had he fared?

I prayed that he had, like me, been able to save himself from the clutches of his captor.

The forest was quiet for a moment, then I heard a tremendous crash to my right.

I ran in the direction of the sound and discovered the corpse of the Jihadoo which had borne me here. It appeared to have died of its wounds.

I shuddered as I looked at the ghastly half-beast and decided that my best plan was to climb a tree quickly again to see if I could catch sight of Hool Haji.

Up the nearest tree I clambered until I was looking over the tops of the foliage.

I saw a speck in the distance, then another – flying creatures, but so far away that I could not make out whether they were Jihadoo or, indeed, if they carried anyone with them.

With a sinking heart I returned to the ground. Somehow I

65

had to discover the lair of the Jihadoo and set off to rescue my friend, hoping that they would not kill him immediately.

But how?

That was a question my mind refused to answer.

I wondered if the cat-girl who had first helped us would be able to help us again if I managed to contact her. I decided that to seek her out was the best thing I could do, and I set off in the general direction of the Crystal Pit.

Even if I did not find the cat-girl, I might be able to capture a dog-man and get the information I needed from him.

Chapter Ten

THE PEOPLE OF PURHA

I MUST have walked for many *shatis* – the Martian basic measure of time – crossing the rocky plain where Rokin had crashed to his death, and entering the next stretch of the forest before I heard some sign of life.

It was a crashing noise in the undergrowth.

It was the sound of some large beast moving about.

Deciding to be cautious, I drew my sword and withdrew into the shade of a bole.

Suddenly, from out of the forest, came yet another weird sight – again almost unbelievable, though this time because the creature bore such a peculiar resemblance to an earthly animal.

The animal that I confronted, and whose gleaming eyes had fixed on me in spite of my attempt at seeking cover, was almost identical to an earth vole.

But this vole was large. It was very large.

It was the size of a half-grown elephant.

And it was hungry – and doubtless omnivorous.

It stood hunched up, regarding me with its nose twitching and its eyes glittering, preparing perhaps for a spring.

I was so weary, what with my experiences since Cend-Amrid and the walking I had done to get this far, that I gave myself only a faint chance of having the strength to defeat the giant vole.

Suddenly, with a peculiar shrill scream, the creature rushed at me. I ducked behind the tree and this seemed to confuse it for a moment.

It plainly was not particularly intelligent, which relieved me a little – though its bulk, I felt, would be more to its advantage in my present state of weariness than my wits would be to me.

For a moment it paused. Then it began to edge round the tree again.

I edged, also, following the trunk of the tree and keeping it between myself and the gigantic creature that was doubtless bent on making a supper from me.

Suddenly it made a movement towards the tree, flinging its huge body at it. The tree groaned and swayed and I was spun backwards, lying helplessly, for a moment, on the ground.

I began to scramble up as the vole came towards me, its relatively small jaws open ready to seize me in a bite that would have severed any part of my body it snapped.

I slashed at the muzzle with my sword, staggering wearily, my vision focusing and unfocusing as I strove to gather what little strength I had left.

The teeth only narrowly missed. I could not run, for the massive creature was faster than I was, and I knew I would not be able to hold it off much longer.

I knew that I was going to die.

Perhaps this knowledge helped me summon my last reserves of strength, and I slashed again at the muzzle, drawing blood. The creature seemed puzzled but it did not retreat, simply holding its ground while it decided how best to attack me.

Again I swayed with utter tiredness, striving with everything I had left to remain on my feet and die fighting.

Then, from above and behind the creature, a rain of slender arrows came pounding into the gigantic vole's body, causing it to scream and convulse in agony. Several arrows whipped into its eyes as it turned towards its new attackers.

I really thought I must be dreaming, that my ill-luck could not have changed so rapidly.

The vole screeched and flailed about. I was knocked flat by its lashing tail as it turned about and began its death throes.

I lay on the springy grass, wide-eyed for a moment, thanking providence for my rescue and praying that I was not to fall into the hands of yet another tribe of barbarians.

As if in the distance, I heard soft voices talking, and had the vision of graceful figures leaping around the dying vole. They gave the impression of cats and, before I finally lost grip on consciousness, I remember reflecting on the paradox of a number of cats attacking a huge mouse!

Then welcome darkness came. Perhaps I had passed out, perhaps not – perhaps I merely slept.

I awoke to the touch of a warm, gentle hand on my head and, opening my eyes, I looked up into the face of the cat-girl who had originally been responsible for my salvation.

"What happened?" I asked somewhat thickly.

"We hunted the *rheti* and found our prey," she replied softly. "Our prey hunted you – and we were able to slay the *rheti* and save you at the same time. Where are your friends?"

I shook my head. "One was killed by the First Masters," I replied. "The other was borne off by them, I think. I do not know how he fared."

"You fought the First Masters and lived!" Her eyes shone with admiration – and something else. "This is a great day. All we had hoped for when I brought you the swords was that you would be able to die fighting. You will be a hero among our folk."

"I have no wish to be a hero," I told her. "Merely a live man – and one who, with luck, still has a chance to find his vanished friend."

"Which friend was carried off?" she asked.

"The Blue Giant – Hool Haji, my closest friend."

"There is little hope for him," she said.

"But is there any?"

"Now now – the First Masters would have feasted last night."

"Last night!" I sat up. "How long have I slept?"

"For nearly two days," she said simply. "You were very weary when we brought you here."

"Two days! So long!"

"It is not so long considering what you did."

"But too long," I said, "for I lost my chance to save Hool Haji."

"You would never have reached the place of the First Masters in time, whatever you did," she soothed. "Salute your friend as a valiant hero. Remember how he died and what that means to those who have suffered the tyranny of the First Masters all these centuries."

"I know that I cannot truthfully blame myself for Hool

69

Haji's death," I said, controlling the emotion I felt at my great friend's passing, "but that does not stop me mourning him."

"Mourn him if you will, but honour him also. He slew many of the First Masters. Never was such a battle fought in the Crystal Pit. Even now the corpses of the First Masters pile its floor. Half of them, at least, lie dead. Tell me of the fight."

As briefly as I could, I told her what had happened.

Her eyes began to shine even more brightly and she clasped her hands together.

"What a great story for our poets!" she gasped. "Oh, what is your name, hero – and the names of your friends?"

"My friends were called the Bradhi Hool Haji of Mendishar from across the ocean, and" – I paused, for Rokin had been no real friend to me, though a valiant comrade in arms in our fights – "the Bradhi Rokin the Gold of the Bagarad."

"Bradhis!" she cried. "And you? What are you – a Bradhi of Bradhis? You could be no less."

I smiled at her enthusiasm. "No," I said. "My name is Michael Kane, Bradhinak by marriage to the Royal House of Varnal that lies far to the South, across the sea."

"From the South – from across the sea. I have heard tales of those mythical lands, the countries of the gods. There are no gods here. They have abandoned us. Are they returning to save us from the First Masters?"

"I am no god," I told her, "and we of the South do not believe in gods. We believe in Man."

"But is not Man a kind of god?" she asked innocently.

I smiled again. "So he sometimes thinks. But the men of my land are not supernatural creatures. They are like you, of flesh and blood and brain. You are no different, though your ancestry is not the same as ours."

"That is not what the First Masters told us."

"The First Masters can speak?" I was astonished. "I thought them reasonless beasts."

"They do not speak to us now. But they left their writings and it is these we read and these we used to follow. The folk of Hahg still worship the First Masters, but we do not."

"Why do they worship the First Masters? I should have thought they would have fought such creatures," I said.

"The First Masters created us," she said simply.

"Created you – but how?"

"We know not how – save for a few scraps of stories that speak of the First Masters as once having served even earlier masters, a race of great magicians who have now passed from Vashu."

I guessed that she spoke of the Sheev or the Yaksha, who had once ruled the whole of Mars – or Vashu, as they called it. Perhaps the winged blue men who had fled from Mendishar in the old days had sought out some remnant of the older race and learned some of their science.

"What do your stories tell you of the First Masters?" I asked.

"They say that the First Masters created our ancestors by putting spells on their brains and shaping their bodies so that they thought and walked like men. For a while our folk – the people of Purha – and the other folk – the people of Hahg – dwelled together in the City of the First Masters, serving them and being sacrificed for their magical purposes."

This sounded like a particularly horrific form of vivisection to me. I interpreted the cat-girl's story in more scientific terms. The First Masters had learned science from an even older race. They had applied it, perhaps by some form of sophisticated surgery, to creating man-like creatures from cats and dogs. Then they had used their creations both as slaves and subjects for their experiments.

"And what happened then?" I asked. "How did the three peoples become separated."

She frowned. "It is hard to understand," she said. "But the minds of the First Masters turned more and more in upon themselves. The magic they had discovered by sacrificing us was applied to their own brains and bodies. They became ... like animals. A madness overcame them. They left their city and flew to their caverns in the mountains far from here. But every five hundred *shatis* they return to the Crystal Pit – a creation either of their own or of the old ones they served – to feed."

"What is their usual food?" I asked.

"Us," she said bleakly.

71

I was disgusted. I could partly understand a psychology that allowed the dog-men of Hahg to sacrifice strangers to their strange masters, but I could only loathe the mentality that let them hurl their cousins, the cat-folk, into the Crystal Pit.

"They eat the people of Purha!" I shuddered.

"Not just the folk of Purha." She shook her head. "Only when the men of Hahg capture us. When they have no prisoners they select the weakest among themselves to provide the food of the First Masters."

"But what inspires them to commit such dreadful crimes!" I gasped.

Again the girl's answer was simple and, it seemed to me, quite profound.

"Fear," she said.

I nodded, wondering if that deep emotion was not the essential cause of most ills. Were not all political systems, all arts, all human actions channelled towards creating that one valuable sense of security we all, in our own ways, sought – an absence of fear? It was fear that produced madness, fear that produced war. Fear, indeed, that often produced the things we feared most. Was this why the fearless man was lauded – because he did not represent a threat to others? Perhaps, though there were many kinds of fearless people, and a total fearlessness produced a whole man, a man who had no need to display his fearlessness. The true hero, in fact – the often unsung hero.

"But there are more of you in one of your tribes than exist among the First Masters," I said. "Why do you not band together to defeat them?"

"The fear the First Masters exert is not on account of their numbers," she replied. "Nor on account of their physical strangeness, though that may have something to do with it. The fear goes deeper. I cannot explain it."

I thought perhaps I knew what she meant. We call it by a simple term on Earth. We call it fear of the unknown. Sometimes it is a man's fear of a woman whom he feels he cannot understand; sometimes it is a man's fear of strangers – of people of a different racial type, or even from a different part

72

of his own land. Sometimes it is fear of the machines that he manipulates. Whether the lack of understanding is on a personal plane or a more general one, it creates suspicion and fear. It was their fear, I thought, not their antecedents that made the dog-men of Hahg something less than human.

I said some of this to the cat-girl and she nodded intelligently. "I think you are right," she said. "Perhaps that is why we survive and grow and the dog-men revert more and more to becoming like their ancestors."

I was struck by her quick brain. Though I hesitate to make such judgments about animals, it seemed to me that the essential cowardice of the dog and the essential courage of the cat might be reflected in the types which had developed from them. Thus I could not blame the dog-men for their brutality quite so much, though this did not alter my deep loathing for what they had become. For, I thought, just as there could be courageous dogs – on Earth there were many stories about them – so could these people have once *found* courage.

I am an optimist, and it occurred to me that just as I might eventually find a means of curing the plague infecting Cend-Amrid, I might also help the dog-men by destroying the cause of their fear – for there was certainly no hope for the First Masters. They were evil. Evil is only another word for what we fear. Go to your Bible if you wish to see the fear of women that inspired the old prophets to call them evil – and evil creates evil. Destroy the first source and there is hope for the rest.

Again I mentioned some of this to the cat-girl. She frowned and nodded. "It is hard to sympathize at all with the men of Hahg," she said. "For what they have done to us in the past has been terrible. But I will try to understand you, Michael Kane."

She got up from where she had been sitting cross-legged beside me.

"My name is Fasa," she said. "Come, see where we live."

She led me from the building in which I had been lying in semi-darkness and had been unable to observe clearly, out into a miniature city built among the trees. Not a tree had been cut in the building of the cat-folk's city. It merged with the forest, thus offering a much subtler kind of protection than the more commonplace clearing and fence used by most jungle-dwelling tribes.

The dwellings were only of one or two stories, fashioned from mud, but mud fashioned into beauty. Here were tiny spires and minarets, painted decorations in pale, lovely colours, a blending of pleasing shapes and colours amongst nature's rich creations.

Some of the darkness in my mind was cleared by the vision and Fasa looked up at me, delighted to see how fascinated I was by the beauty of her settlement.

"You like it?"

"I love it," I said enthusiastically. In its own simple way it reminded me of Varnal of the Green Mists more than anything else I had seen on Mars. It had the same air of tranquillity – a vital tranquillity, if you like – which made me feel so much at home and at ease in Varnal.

"You are an artistic people," I said, fingering the sword which I still wore. "I saw that at once when you first brought us these blades."

"We try," she said. "I sometimes think that if the surroundings can be made pleasing they help the soul."

Again I was struck by the simple profundities – common sense, if you prefer – coming from this beautiful girl. But what is the deepest wisdom but the soundest kind of common sense, *true* common sense? Living in isolated conditions, beset by enemies of two kinds, these cat-people seemed to have something more valuable than most nations, even on Mars and certainly on Earth.

"Come," she said, taking my arm. "You must meet my old uncle, Slurra. He will like you, I think, Michael Kane. He already admires you – but admiration does not always produce liking, wouldn't you say?"

"I agree," I said feelingly, and let her lead me towards one of the beautiful buildings.

I had to duck my head to enter and there I saw an old cat-man, sitting relaxed and at ease in a delicately carved chair. He did not rise as I entered, but his expression and his inclination of the head seemed more to respect me than any empty gesture of politeness I might have received on Earth.

"We were not aware of the benefits we would bring to the people of Purha when we sent Fasa to you with the swords," he said.

"Benefits?" I enquired.

"Immeasurable ones," he said, gesturing for me to sit in a chair close to him. "To see the First Masters defeated – and they *were* defeated in a deeper sense than you may realize – to be shown that they could be killed, was the thing my folk needed most."

"Perhaps," I said, nodding agreement to show that I knew what he meant, "this will help the Hahg, also."

He debated this for a moment before replying. "Yes, it might, if they have not gone too far down the road. It will make them sceptical of the First Masters' power, just as we became sceptical long years ago, well before my great-grandfather's time, in the age of Mispash the Founder."

"A wise man of your folk?" I enquired.

"The founder of our folk," replied the old cat-man. "He taught us one great truth – he was the wisest of prophets."

"What was that?"

"Never to seek prophets," Slurra smiled. "One should be enough – and he a wise one."

I reflected how true this was and how well Slurra's words applied to the situation on Earth where, because prophets had been found, whole nations now sought new prophets rather than study the teachings of the few whose universal message had always been, *know thyself*. Not knowing themselves, perhaps even fearing to, these nations allowed artificial prophets – Adolf Hitler was an example who came to mind at once – to cure their ills. All such prophets did was to plunge those who listened to them into a worse situation than any they had been in before.

I talked at some length with the old cat-man and found the conversation rewarding.

Then he said: "But all this is fine enough. We must do something to help you."

75

"Thank you," I said.

"What can we do?"

I remembered the machines left behind in the beached ship. That would be my first objective, I decided. If the cat-people could help me it would make things much easier. I told the old cat-man, Slurra, of the reasons for my being here.

He listened gravely and when I had finished he said: "You have a noble mission, Michael Kane. We should be proud to help you carry it out. As soon as you are ready, there will be a party of my people to come with you to this ship and the machines can be brought back here."

"Are you sure you want these fated machines among you?" I asked.

"Machines are only dangerous, I believe, in the hands of dangerous men. It is such men we must be wary of, not their tools," said Slurra. I had already explained the power and implications of the ancient machines.

And so it was agreed. In a short time an expedition, led by me, would set off for the coast.

It was not my intention to engage the cat-folk in battle with the barbarians – or, indeed, to set out to harm the barbarians, who had been led into danger by Rokin. I hoped that a display of strength and some sensible words, coupled with the information that Rokin was now dead, would encourage them to fall in with us.

Things were not to happen quite like that, but I did not realize it at the time.

Chapter Eleven

"THE MACHINES ARE GONE!"

IT took us some time to reach the coast, and a little longer to retrace my steps to where I had left the ship.

As we neared the ship I noticed that something seemed wrong. No guards moved on the deck, all appeared as still as the grave.

I began to trot faster, the cat-men following me. There were some twenty of them, well armed with bows and swords, and they hardly realized what a tremendous comfort they were to me on this Western continent.

When I reached the ship I saw signs that some kind of fight had taken place.

Two dead barbarians were next revealed, savagely beaten to death.

Zapha, the captain commanding the cat-men, inspected the ground. Then his intelligent cat's face looked up at me thoughtfully.

"More victims for the First Masters, if I'm not mistaken, Michael Kane," he said. "The men of Hahg have been here – they have taken prisoners."

"They must be saved," I said grimly.

He shook his head. "The men of Hahg must have wondered where you came from and followed your trucks back. This happened two days ago. The First Masters will not go back to the Crystal Pit yet, but you were only saved from the sport of the men of Hahg because your appearance coincided with the latest visit of the First Masters."

"What sport is that?"

"A grisly one – torture of a dreadful kind. I do not think you will find your friends alive in the mind now – though they'll live until the next visit of the First Masters."

I felt horrified and then depressed. "Still, we shall have to do what we can," I said firmly.

I clambered up the side of the ship and walked across the sloping deck towards the hold where I knew the machines were stored.

I looked down.

I saw nothing but brackish water.

"The machines are gone!" I cried, running back to the broken rail and calling to the cat-men.

"The machines are gone!"

Zapha looked up at me with surprise in his eyes. "They have taken them? It is not like them to do anything but capture victims for the First Masters."

"Nonetheless, they are gone," I said, climbing down the side of the ship.

"Then we must hurry back to the village of the Hahg and see if we can recover them," Zapha said boldly.

We turned and began to go back the way we had come.

"We must get additional forces before we do that," I said.

"Perhaps," said Zapha thoughtfully. "But this number has been enough in the past."

"You have attacked the Hahg before?"

"When necessary – to save our own folk usually."

"I cannot draw you into this fight," I said.

"Do not worry. This fight is ours and yours – it is linked because the cause is common," said Zapha firmly.

I respected his words and understood his feelings.

Thus we set off hurriedly for the Hahg encampment.

As we neared the encampment, Zapha and his followers began to show more caution and Zapha signed to me to follow him.

I could not move with the grace of the cat-folk, who now advanced completely silently through the forest, but I did my best.

Soon we lay in the undergrowth, peering at the squalid Hahg village, which, I had learned, was built on the ruins left behind by the First Masters when they had gone to the mountains.

From somewhere we heard mindless cries of agony and I knew what they signified.

This time Zapha stayed my hand as, impulsively, I made to rise.

"Not yet," he said, only just audibly.

I remembered a similar warning I had given Hool Haji and realized that Zapha was right. Action we would take – but only at the right moment.

Looking about the camp I suddenly saw the machines. They were surrounded by a group of grunting dog-men, who were poking at them in what appeared to be mystification.

What impulse had led them to go to the trouble of hauling the machines here? Some atavistic memory? Some association with the First Masters whom they tried, at such pitiful and inhuman cost, to please?

Perhaps that was half the answer. I did not know.

The fact remained that here they were and we must somehow recapture them. We must also rescue what remained of the tortured barbarians.

Suddenly there came a disturbance in the air above us and I was astonished to see the First Masters descending into the village.

Zapha was as astonished as I was.

"Why are they here?" I whispered. "Surely they only go to the Crystal Pit to feed every five hundred *shatis*?"

"I cannot imagine," Zapha said. "We are witnessing something important, I think, Michael Kane, though I cannot understand at this point what it signifies!"

With a great noise of leathery, beating wings, the First Masters landed near the machines and the dog-folk withdrew obsequiously.

Again I got the impression of some atavistic impulse working in the First Masters as they strutted, like stupid birds of prey, among the machines.

Suddenly one of them reached out and touched part of a machine that seemed to me merely ornamentation. Immediately a weird humming began to fill the air and the machine that had been activated began to shudder.

The dog-folk cowered back. Then the First Master who had originally touched the activating stud touched it again. The humming ceased.

As it disturbed by this, the First Masters began to take to the air again, disappearing as rapidly and as mysteriously as they had come.

We watched as the dog-people slowly returned to sniff at the machines.

The pack-leader barked out some kind of order. The vines which had been used to haul the machines to the village were picked up and the dog-men began pulling them away in the opposite direction.

"Where are they taking them?" I whispered to Zapha.

"I only heard a little of what the leader said," replied Zapha. "I think they are going to the Crystal Pit."

"They are taking the machines there? I wonder why."

"It does not matter at this moment, Michael Kane. What does matter is that they are leaving the village almost undefended. This will give us a chance to rescue your friends first."

I did not quarrel with his description of the barbarians. They had been no real friends to me, but I felt I owed them something as human beings who had shown their prisoners at least some kind of rough respect.

We walked boldly into the village when the dog-men hauling the machines had gone. Those who remained saw that we outnumbered them and allowed their women and children to draw them back into their dark shelters.

Poor creatures! Cowardice had become their way of life.

The cat-folk did not bother them, but went to the shelter from where the moans had come earlier. There were none now and I assumed the barbarians had passed out.

But the two barbarians in the shelter had not passed out.

They had killed themselves.

From the beam of the shelter a rope hung. It had been looped over and a noose formed at either end.

Hanging, with their necks in the nooses, were the two barbarians.

I leapt forward with the idea of cutting them down but Zapha shook his head.

"They are dead," he said. "Perhaps it is best."

"I am tempted to avenge them here and now," I said harshly, turning towards the entrance.

"It was you who told us of the real cause of all this, Michael Kane," Zapha reminded me.

I controlled my emotions and left the place of death.

Zapha came out with me.

"Let us follow the Hahg to the Crystal Pit now," he said. "We might learn something. Perhaps that is where the First Masters have gone, too."

I agreed, and we left the village and the stench of fear behind us.

Chapter Twelve

THE DANCE OF THE FIRST MASTERS

THE long grass hid our approach up to the Crystal Pit and we lay observing the weird sight before us.

The dog-people had by this time almost dragged the machines up to the brink of the scintillating pit.

I watched, uncertain what to do, as they heaved them over the edge. I heard them slide down, some of them seeming to protest with a screaming noise created by the friction as they slid into the pit.

Just as they had done with us, the dog-people began to back away from the edge once the last machine had been deposited. I knew that the Yaksha machines were durable enough not to have been harmed by the way they had been handled.

Then, in the distance, I saw the First Masters come winging to settle into the pit like vultures upon a corpse.

For a moment all of them were obscured from our view by the sides of the pit; then they came flapping up again, in some sort of order, until they had formed a circle, hovering again in the air above the Crystal Pit.

Now they began to perform a weird, aerial dance, following a pattern which I could not at once understand.

The dance went on, becoming more and more frenetic, and yet keeping its order, no matter how fast the First Masters flew.

There was something almost pathetic about this dance and, not for the first time, I could sympathize a little with the long forgotten impulses which had driven the First Masters to become the mindless things they now were.

On and on went the dance of the First Masters; faster and faster they whirled in the air above the Crystal Pit. Whether it was a ritual of homage to the machines or a dance of hatred I shall never know.

What I do know, however, is that some of their insensate

emotion was reflected in me, and I watched in awe as it went on.

Finally one of their number dived swiftly into the pit. A second followed, then another and yet another, until all were once again hidden from our view.

I assumed that they must have activated something in the machines.

Suddenly there came a vast eruption from the Crystal Pit, a pillar of fire that rose hundreds of feet into the air.

The atmosphere was torn by a great, screaming roar. The dog-people had not had time to retreat to a safe distance. Every one of them was consumed in the blast of energy from the pit.

For a few moments the pillar of fire continued to rise higher and higher. Then it subsided.

The air was still.

Nothing moved.

Zapha and the other cat-folk said nothing. We simply exchanged glances that showed our deep bewilderment at what we had just witnessed.

There was no longer any possibility of discovering if one of the machines was the one I needed. I would just have to hope that the one I wanted – if it still existed – survived somewhere else.

The First Masters were dead, taking most of their servants with them.

Back in the cat village, we told the folk of Purha what we had seen.

There was an atmosphere of quiet jubilation about the village then, though the cat-people were contemplative enough to brood on the significance of what we told them – though its true significance was hard to fathom.

Some death-wish had been tapped in the First Masters, some ancient drive which had taken them to the destruction of themselves as human beings – and now as entities.

A cycle seemed to have been completed. It would be best to forget it, I felt.

My next objective must be to find Bagarad.

There the other stolen machines remained – or so I hoped.

There I might find what I sought.

I discussed this with the cat-people and they told me that they felt it their duty to go with me to Bagarad. I told them that their company would be welcome, particularly since I still mourned the loss of Hool Haji. But I did not wish to get them involved in any fighting.

"Let *us* decide whether the fighting should involve us or not," said Zapha with a quiet smile.

Fasa now spoke up. "I would go with you, Michael Kane, but it is hard for me to leave at the moment. Take this, however, and hope it brings you luck."

She handed to me a needle-thin dagger which could be fitted behind my harness. In some ways it resembled the hidden skinning knife of the Mendishar and it was intended to be used for the same purpose – if danger threatened.

I accepted it gratefully, commenting on the weapon's precise workmanship.

"A little rest," I said, "if I may, and we'll be off to seek Bagarad."

The wise old cat-man, Slurra, brought out some tablets which he had told me of earlier.

"Here is the only map we have," he said. "It is probably inexact, but it still show you the general direction to take in order to reach the country of the barbarians."

I accepted this also with an expression of thanks. He raised his hand.

"Do not thank us – let us thank you that we can repay all you have done for us, both with your actions and your words," he said. "I only hope that you will return to Purha some day, when the world is tranquil."

"It will be one of the first things I shall do," I promised, "if I ever accomplish my mission and remain alive."

"If it is possible, Michael Kane, you will do it – and live." He smiled.

Next morning, myself, Zapha and a party of cat-men set off for Bagarad, which lay to the south of the land of the cat-people.

Our journey was a long one, and involved crossing a

mountain range where, to our sorrow, we lost one of our number.

But on the other side of the valley we encountered a land of friendly, farming folk who willingly gave us daharas in exchange for some of the cat-folk's artifacts, which they had brought along for this purpose.

The cat-folk were not used to riding, but their quick intelligence and sense of balance helped, and soon we were all riding along like old cavalrymen!

The going was fairly easy for several days until we came to a land of marshes and lowering skies. Here we had difficulty picking our way along the ribbons of firm ground which crisscrossed the marshes.

It seemed to be drizzling permanently and it was much colder.

I would be glad when we left this area and found a pleasanter land.

We spoke little as we rode, concentrating on guiding our daharas through the marshes.

It was towards evening on the third day of our journey through the marsh when we first discovered we were being watched.

Zapha, with his quick cat's eyes, noticed it first and rode up to warn me.

"I have only seen glimpses of them," he said, "but there are a number of men out there in the marsh. We had better be wary of attack."

Then I began to notice them and began to feel uncomfortable.

It was not until night had fallen that they suddenly rose from all around us and came silently towards us. They were tall men, well-shaped but for their heads, which were smaller than they should have been in proportion to their bodies.

They bore swords – heavy, wide-bladed affairs which they swung at us and which we met with our lighter weapons.

We were able to defend ourselves well enough, but in the darkness it was confusing, for these people evidently knew the marsh and we did not.

I struck about me, keeping them at a distance, my dahara

rearing and snorting and becoming difficult to control. These beasts were harder to control than the variety found on Southern Mars and part of my concentration had to be used to quiet my beast as best I could.

I felt a blade nick my arm, but paid little attention to the wound.

Through the darkness I caught glimpses of my comrades fighting, and every so often one would go down. So I decided that it would be best if we made a dash for it, hoping to keep firm ground under our beasts' feet.

I shouted to Zapha and he yelled back his agreement. We urged our daharas forward and began to gallop recklessly away from the men who had attacked us.

On through the night we rode, praying that the swamp would not take us. The small-headed men behind us appeared to give up the chase quite soon, and at length we were able to slow down. We decided that, since the moons had risen, we should continue rather than make camp and risk a further attack at night.

By morning we were still safe, although once or twice we had narrowly escaped riding into the marsh, and were very tired.

My wound was aching a little, but I soon bound it up and forgot about it. We were now near the edge of the marsh and could see firmer ground ahead of us.

Also we could see the outlines of what appeared to be a series of buildings, but it was hard to decide whether they comprised a city or not.

Zapha suggested that we should approach the place cautiously, but he also thought that it would be a safe place to make camp if it were uninhabited.

As we approached the buildings we noticed that they were, in fact, ruined shells of houses. Weeds grew in the streets. It looked as if, long ago, a fire had destroyed the city.

But when we approached closer we saw a party of mounted men to the west of the city. They were riding full tilt at it with bared weapons – swords and axes mainly. They were yellow-skinned men and were wearing bright cloaks and highly-decorated war-harness. The yellow of their skins was not like that of the Oriental, but a deeper, brighter yellow, somewhat like lemon-yellow.

From somewhere within the ruins we heard a yell – the voice of one man – and we gathered that it was he the yellow men were attacking.

We were undecided how to act, not knowing what situation had arisen, but rode in closer to get a better view of what was happening.

Then I saw the man whose voice we had heard – and I could not believe my eyes.

The man whom the yellow warriors attacked with such ferocity was none other than Hool Haji!

The Blue Giant looked weary and travel-stained. He seemed to have a half-healed wound in his shoulder, but he bore a great, wide sword of a kind I had seen in the hands of the yellow-skinned warriors.

As the yellow riders bore down on Hool Haji, I gave a great shout and urged my dahara towards him.

Zapha and his men followed and soon we were face to face with the yellow warriors.

They seemed dismayed by our sudden appearance. They had expected to have to fight only one man and now found nearly twenty riders coming to his rescue.

We had killed and wounded only a few before the rest turned their mounts about and rode away. They mounted a hill and were quickly lost from our view on the other side.

I swung myself off my dahara's broad back and walked towards Hool Haji. He seemed as astonished to see me as I was to see him.

"Hool Haji!" I cried. "You are alive! How did you get here?"

He laughed. "You will think me a liar when I tell you – but tell you I must. I had thought you dead, also, Michael Kane. Have you any food? We must feast and celebrate our coming together again!"

We posted guards and the rest of us built a fire and cooked some provisions.

While we ate, Hool Haji told me his story.

He had, as I suspected, been carried to the mountain lair

87

of the First Masters. It was a dark warren of caves in the highest peaks and there they nested like strange birds.

He had not been harmed at first, but had been deposited close to the central nest, where a young creature of the same species rested.

From the way that they protected this youngster, Hool Haji gathered that this was, in fact, the last of their species, since he saw no females while he was there.

He had been left as food for the young one by the First Masters and expected them to kill him but, just as they were coming towards him, something had disturbed them. He didn't know what it was. They had suddenly taken it into their heads to fly off.

Left alone with the young one, who was actually not very much smaller than himself, he had conceived the idea of training it and thus escaping from the eyrie.

Using his sword, which the First Masters had not had sense enough to take from him, he prodded the young creature to the edge of the outer cage. He clambered upon its back and, by many pricks from the sword, had taught it to obey him.

He had meant to return in the direction of the Crystal Pit and see if he could find any trace of me, but the young Jihadoo – as Hool Haji called it – had revealed a mind of its own after its initial bewilderment, and had resisted him.

It had begun to fly very fast until it had become very tired.

Lower and lower it had sunk, by this time just managing to brush over the tops of the trees.

Then some kind of weariness caused it to turn in the air and begin snapping at Hool Haji. A fight developed. Hool Haji was forced to kill the creature to protect himself and they had both fallen to earth, where Hool Haji had escaped with only a few bruises. But the creature was dead.

Hool Haji had landed in the swamp we had just crossed, but had managed to haul himself to firm ground, and began crossing the marsh.

Then the men with small heads had attacked. Hool Haji called them the Perodi.

They had overwhelmed him after a desperate fight and

taken him overland to a city which lay many *shatis* to the West.

Here the men with small heads had sold him as a slave to the yellow-skinned people who lived in the city – the Cinivik, as they called themselves.

Hool Haji had refused to work as a slave for the Cinivik and had at length been chained in one of their prisons, of which, apparently, they had many.

He was displayed, because of his physical peculiarities, as some kind of zoo specimen, but bided his time until he had recovered all his strength.

Then he had managed to wrench his chains out of the wall and throttle his gaoler, taking the man's sword and escaping, after a fight or two, from the city.

As luck would have it, his only route of escape was into the marshes. He had had several encounters with the Perodi but had managed to beat them. He had won several swords from them in these fights and had snapped two while getting the chains off his arm.

Apparently a reward had been offered for him and the Perodi had told the Cinivik where he was. He had taken to using the ruins as his main base.

A small party of warriors had been sent out to find him, but he had killed several and beaten the rest off.

He would have been killed or recaptured, he believed, if we had not arrived on the scene just as the second expedition were about to attack him.

"And that, in brief, is the sum total of my adventures until today," he told me. "I am sorry if I have bored you."

"You have not," I told him. "And now let me tell you my story. I think you will like it."

I told Hool Haji everything that had happened since our forced parting and he listened attentively.

After I had finished, he said: "Of the two of us, the most has happened to you. So you are on the way to Bagarad now, are you? I will be pleased to rejoin you and help as best I can."

"Discovering you alive is the best thing that has happened yet," I told him sincerely.

That night I slept well and deeply.

In the morning we rode on for Bagarad, which was still several days' journey away.

The terrain was easier now and made travel lighter. The whole party of us rode long, talking and joking among ourselves, while a great plain stretched away in all directions, giving us a sense of security, since no enemies could approach without warning.

But there were no enemies on the plain, only herds of strange looking animals which, Zapha informed us, were quite harmless.

Soon the plain gave way to hill country that was just as pleasant, for the hills were covered in bright, orange grass, with red and yellow flowers growing in profusion.

It was strange how, on Mars, one would discover a landscape quite similar to Earth's and then, suddenly, come upon another that one might never expect to find on any planet.

Soon now, if the map was accurate, we should come to Bagarad and the long-missing machines.

Chapter Thirteen

THE REMAINS

By the next afternoon we had left the hills and were crossing a rugged landscape of rock and coarse turf, with twisted trees springing from anywhere that a little earth had deposited itself amongst cracks in the rocks.

This was the land where Bagarad lay.

But before we reached Bagarad we came upon a party of barbarians whom I recognized as being similar to those who had followed Rokin to eventual destruction.

They were gaunt-eyed men, women and children – and they merely waited for us to pass without challenging us in any way.

I stopped my dahara and spoke to one of them.

"Do you know where Bagarad lies from here?" I asked.

The man mumbled something which I did not catch.

"I do not hear you," I said.

"Do not look for Bagarad," he said. "If you would see where Bagarad lies, go that way." And he pointed.

I was a little perturbed by what he had said, but set my dahara in the direction he had indicated. Hool Haji, Zapha, and the cat-men followed.

It was nearly evening by the time we came to Bagarad.

There was very little of it left.

There were only ruins and the ruins were deserted. A pall of dusty smoke hung over them.

I knew instinctively what had happened. We had come too late. The barbarians had tampered with the machines and destroyed themselves.

Those we had seen must have been the remnants who had survived.

I climbed down from my dahara and began to pick my way through the ruins.

Here was a piece of metal, there part of a coil. It was

evident that all the Yaksha machines had been destroyed.

I noticed a small metal tube and picked it up. It must have been a part from one of the machines. I tucked it into my belt-pouch regretfully – it was the only complete part left.

With a sigh I turned turned to Hool Haji.

"Well, my friend," I said, "our quest is over. Somehow we must now return to the Yaksha vaults to see if anything remains."

Hool Haji clasped my shoulder. "Do not worry, Michael Kane. Perhaps it was for the best that the machines were destroyed."

"Unless one of them held the secret that could have cured the plague," I pointed out. "Think of the madness and the misery in Cend-Amrid. How are we going to combat that?"

"We must simply put the case to our physicians and hope they can devise a cure."

But I shook my head. "Martian physicians are not used to analysing diseases. There is no cure for the Green Death – or will not be for many years."

"I suppose you are right," he admitted. "Then the Yaksha vaults are our only chance."

"It seems to be so."

"But how are we to return to our own continent?" was his next question.

"We must find a ship." I pointed to the east, where the sea could be seen in the distance.

"Finding a ship is not so easy," Hool Haji said.

"The Bagarad had ships," I told him. "They must have a harbour." I pulled out a map. "Look. There is a river not far from here. Perhaps they have ships moored there."

"Let us go there, then," he said. "I am aching to set foot in my own land again."

We rode to the river and, after a while, we discovered a place where several Bagarad ships were moored. They were deserted.

What urge had made the survivors go inland? I wondered. Why had they not taken a ship? Perhaps they associated ships with the machines that had destroyed their city. I could think of no other explanation.

We decided on a small ship with a single mast that could just about be worked by two men.

Zapha spoke to me after Hool Haji had picked out our boat and we had discussed its merits.

"Michael Kane," said Zapha, "we would be honoured if you would take us with you."

I shook my head. "You have helped enough, Zapha. You will be needed by your own people, and it is a long journey back. In a way, your journey has been wasted, but I am glad you have lost so few men."

"That is a relief to me, too," he said. "But ... but we would follow you, Michael Kane. We still feel our debt to you."

"Do not thank me," I told him. "Thank circumstances. It could have been any other man."

"I do not think so."

"Be careful, Zapha," I said. "Remember your old prophet. If you admire something in me, look for it in yourself. You will find it there."

He smiled. "I see what you mean," he said. "Yes, perhaps you are right."

Soon after that we parted regretfully and I hoped that some day I would be able to return to Purha and meet the cat-people again.

Hool Haji and I checked our boat and discovered that it was well provisioned, as if it had been intended for use just before the explosion.

With some misgivings, Hool Haji allowed me to shove off and soon we were sailing down the river, bound for the open sea.

The sea soon loomed ahead of us and at length we had left land behind.

Luckily, the ocean was not in turmoil. Hool Haji said that he thought this was normally a quiet season on the Western ocean, and I thanked providence for that.

We set a course for a part of the coast nearest to the Yaksha vaults.

Was there still time to save Cend-Amrid?

I did not know.

Some days passed and our voyage had been without mishap. We were just beginning to feel that good luck was now completely on our side when Hool Haji gave a startled cry and pointed ahead of us.

There, heaving itself from the deep ocean, was a monster of staggering proportions.

Water ran from its back and dripped from its great, green head. Streamers of flesh clung to its body, as if it had been lacerated in some mighty underwater fight.

It did not seem to be mammal or fish – a reptile perhaps, though its body was like that of a hippopotamus and its head somewhat resembled that of a duck-billed platypus.

It was not so much its appearance as its size that was so astonishing. It dominated our little boat and could have opened its jaws and swallowed it, had it wished.

Perhaps it did not normally come to the surface but had been driven there by the victor of the fight it must recently have had.

Whatever the reason, we wished that it had not come, for it paddled towards us, seemingly motivated more by curiosity than anything else.

We could do nothing but gape and hope that it would not attack us.

The huge head bent and the great eyes gazed and I had the impression, in spite of my fears, that it was not in any way a savage beast.

Indeed, it seemed more gentle than many much smaller creatures I had encountered on Mars.

Having inspected us, it raised its head again and looked about, as if taking a last look at the surface.

Then it began to dive, leaving behind it a foaming sea, perhaps returning to the fray it had left, perhaps simply disturbed by what it had seen.

Hool Haji and I breathed a sigh of relief.

"What was it?" I asked him. "Do you know?"

"I have only heard of it. In Mendishar they call it a Sea Mother – because of its gentle nature, perhaps. They have never been known to harm ships. At least, they have never

94

deliberately attacked one, though occasionally they have sunk one by accident."

"Then I am glad it saw us first." I smiled.

A little later we saw a shoal of large creatures, much smaller than the Sea Mother, but nonetheless daunting, and Hool Haji spoke warningly.

"I hope they do not come too close," he said. "They are by no means as gentle as the Sea Mother."

I could make out their snake-like bodies and their sharp heads, rather like swordfish.

"What are they?" I said.

"*N'heer*," he told me. "They range all the seas in packs, attacking anything they see." He smiled bleakly. "Luckily they don't see as much as they might, since they are extremely short-sighted creatures."

We steered as far away from the *n'heer* as we could get, but it was our bad luck that they should take it into their heads to swim closer and closer to the ship.

Hool Haji drew his sword.

"Be ready," he said softly. "I think they will see us in a moment."

And, sure enough, they did.

They had been moving at a fairly leisurely pace, but now they darted swiftly through the water, their sinuous necks straight out, their pointed heads like so many spears flying at us.

They drove at the ship, but the ancient hull resisted this and for a moment they swam around rapidly in some sort of confusion.

Then they rose further out of the water and began to stab at us.

We slashed at their pointed heads with our swords and they hissed and snapped at us.

Shoulder to shoulder we fought them off as more of them attacked. Our swords pierced their comparatively soft bodies but seemed to have little lasting effect on them.

Some of them had flopped completely out of the water and landed on the deck.

They writhed towards us.

95

One of them managed to stab me in the leg before I ran my sword into its eye.

Another nearly took my arm off, but I chopped its head open.

Soon the deck was slippery with their blood and I found it difficult to keep my footing.

Just when it seemed that we should soon be food for the *n'heer,* I heard the throb of engines above me.

It was an impossible sound.

I risked a glance upwards.

It was an impossible sight!

There were several airships of my own design. From their cabins floated the colours of Varnal.

What freak of chance had brought them here?

I had not time to think of that then, as we were forced to concentrate on defending ourselves against the *n'heer.*

But help came from the airships. Arrows rained down on the slimy creatures and many died before the rest swam rapidly off.

A rope was lowered from one of the ships. I grabbed it and began to climb.

Soon I was looking into the face of none other than my brother by marriage – Darnad of the Varnal. His youthful face was grinning in delight and relief and he gripped my shoulder warmly.

"Michael Kane, my brother!" he said. "At last we have found you!"

"What do you mean?" I asked.

"I will tell you later. Let us help Hool Haji aboard first. Luck has been with you."

As we helped Hool Haji aboard, I was forced to give him an ironic grin. "Luck has been with me? I did not think so until now."

Chapter Fourteen

THE GREEN DEATH

Darnad sat at the controls of the airship I had taught him to navigate and several Varnalian warriors sat around on the couches grinning their joy at seeing us again.

"I would like to know just how you happened to be in this part of the Western ocean at this particular time," I said. "The coincidence seems too incredible to be true."

"It is no coincidence, really," he said, "but happy circumstances."

"Then tell me of them."

"Do you remember a girl from Cend-Amrid? Ala Mara, her name is."

"Of course. But how do you know her?"

"Well, you left her in your airship when you went to inspect the vaults of the Yaksha, did you not?"

"We did."

"Apparently the girl became a little bored and began fiddling with the control panel of the ship. She meant no harm, naturally, but by accident she released the mooring lines of the airship and the craft began to drift in the wind."

"So that is what happened. Lucky for her that it did, I think."

"Why so?"

"Because otherwise she would have been found by those who captured us."

"Who were they?"

"I'll tell you that when I've heard the rest of your story."

"Very well. The airship drifted on the air currents for many days before it was sighted by one of our patrol craft which had set out with a message for you from Shizala."

"A message?"

"Yes. I will also tell you of that in a moment."

"The girl told of the situation in Cend-Amrid and why you had gone to the Yaksha vaults. The ship returned first to

Varnal with the girl and its news. Then I headed this expedition to Yaksha to see if we could help since we guessed you would be almost stranded there without any means of transport – though we thought you might make for Mendishar.

"When we arrived at Mendishar they had no news of you, so we went to Yaksha."

"And found us gone."

"Exactly."

"What did you do then?"

"Well, we did discover signs that many of the machines had been removed. Also, we found the corpses of many warriors whom we did not recognize. We gathered that you had been in a fight and had vanquished your enemies. We guessed then that you might have been captured. Travelling overland, we were able to follow a trail through the desert to the coast where we found further signs that a ship had recently left there."

"What did you do when you discovered that the ship had probably taken us over the sea?"

"There was little we could do, save try to find the ship – and we never did find it. All we could do after that was scour both sea and coast in the hope of finding some clue. We were on our fifth trip back when we sighted your boat and were able to help you."

"In the nick of time," I said. "I'm very grateful, Darnad."

"Nonsense. But what has happened to you? Did you find a machine that will be able to cure the plague?"

"No, I am sorry to say."

Then I told Darnad all that had happened to us. He listened avidly.

"I am glad you both survived," he said. "And I hope we shall all be able to see the cat-people some day."

"Now," I smiled. "I have been patient enough. What was the message being borne to me from Shizala?"

"A joyful one," Darnad said. "You are to become a father!"

That one scrap of news did more for me than anything else. I could hardly contain my enthusiasm, and everyone joined in congratulating me.

It had been worth going through all I had done to hear that

Shizala was going to give me a child. I could not wait to get home and see her.

But first there was my duty. I had to visit the Yaksha vaults and seek the device that the Yaksha must have possessed to counter the effects of the Green Death.

Now we were crossing the land and the Yaksha vaults in the desert would soon be reached.

Then we saw them below us and Darnad brought the airship closer to the ground.

The ships were moored and we left a few men on guard while we once again entered the vaults.

This time, with more men, we could make a really thorough search for the device we sought. For all I knew it might be in tablet or even liquid form, but knowing the fantastically sophisticated science of the Yaksha I thought it might be a machine capable of dispensing some kind of ray that would work directly on the disease germs.

We searched for several days. The vaults were vast, and it took time to check everything we found. The barbarians had left a great deal. They had taken, in fact, only those machines that seemed designed for war. Many other types were left, though all the war machines, it seemed, had gone. Now I knew they were destroyed for good, and perhaps it was just as well, though I regretted missing the opportunity of analysing their principles.

But, though we checked everything, we could find nothing that seemed designed to counter the Green Death. At length we were forced to give up and return to the airships.

Now I sat at the controls while Darnad relaxed.

I set a course for Varnal.

"Now what can we do?" Darnad asked gloomily. "Must we forget Cend-Amrid?"

"If you had seen the horror there," I told him, "you would not suggest that. We shall just have to try to find a cure ourselves, though the time that would take must be very long – unless we are very lucky."

We did not pass over Cend-Amrid on our way back and I

99

was rather relieved, for I did not think I could bear to look on the place, even from such a height.

But it was as we neared the Crimson Plain that lies quite close to Varnal that I noticed a vast procession of people below me,

At first I thought it was an army on the march, but its order was too ragged.

I dropped lower to see it and observed that it was in fact made up of men, women and children of all ages.

I was fascinated by the sight and could not understand why so many people should be on the move.

I guided the airship down lower and then saw in horror what I had half feared since I had left Cend-Amrid.

The Green Death was on them all.

Somehow a traveller must have come and gone from Cend-Amrid and taken the seeds of the plague with him.

Perhaps he had returned to his own city – and it had become infected.

But why were they on the move?

I took the megaphone from its place near the control panel and went to the cabin door.

I shouted down at the crowd, who were by this time gaping up.

They were all in rags, with gaunt, haunted faces.

"Who are you?" I bellowed through the megaphone. "Where are you from?"

One of them shouted back: "We are the non-functional! We seek refuge."

"What do you mean, non-functional? Do you come, then, from Cend-Amrid?"

"Some of us do. But many come from Opquel, Fiola and Ishal, too."

"Who told you you were non-functional?" I shouted. "The folk of Cend-Amrid?"

"We have a mechanic with us. He, too, is non-functional. He is our head – we are his hands, his motor, his feet."

I realized then that not only the plague had come from Cend-Amrid – so had part of the dreadful creed that ruled there.

100

"If he is non-functional, why does he lead you?"

"We are the great non-functional. It is our duty to produce a non-functional world."

I was experiencing a further perversion of logic whereby someone had convinced those infected by the plague that it was good to have the plague and bad not to have it.

This could mean that the Green Death could spread like wildfire throughout Southern Mars – perhaps across the whole planet – unless it could somehow be checked.

"Where do you go now?" I asked.

"Varnal!" came the reply.

I almost dropped the megaphone in horror.

The Green Death must not reach Varnal.

Now I had something even more intensely personal to fight for. Would I keep my head?

I prayed that I would.

"Do not go to Varnal!" I cried, half pleadingly. "Stay where you are! We will find a way of curing you. Do not fear!"

"Cure us!" shouted the man. "Why should you wish to? We are bringing the joys of the Green Death to all men!"

"But the Green Death means horror and agony!" I cried. "How can you believe that it is good?"

"Because it is Death!" replied the man.

"But surely you cannot seek death. You cannot want to die – it is against all that is human!"

"Death brings the cessation of function," droned the plague victim. "Cessation of function is good. The evil man is the functioning man."

I shut the cabin door against him. I leaned back against the walls of the cabin, sweating.

"They must be stopped!" growled Hool Haji, who had overheard most of the conversation.

"How?" I half moaned.

"If it comes to that, we must destroy them," he said bleakly.

"No!" I cried.

But I knew I hardly believed what I said. I was becoming a victim of fear.

I must fight that fear, I knew. But what was I to do?

Chapter Fifteen

THE THREAT TO VARNAL

WE sped as rapidly as we could towards Varnal and at last her slender towers came in sight.

As soon as we had landed I made for the palace and there, waiting on the steps to greet me, was my Shizala, lovely Bradhinaka of the Kanala, loveliest flower of the House of Varnal.

I sprang to embrace her, careless of who saw us.

She returned my embrace and looked into my face with shining eyes.

"Oh, Michael Kane, you are back at last! I had feared you dead, my Bradhinak!"

"I cannot die while you live," I said. "That would be foolish of me."

She smiled at me then.

"Have you heard my news?" she said.

I pretended I had not.

I wished to hear it from her own lips.

"Then come to our apartments," she told me. "And I will tell you there."

In our apartments she told me simply that we were to have a child. It was enough to bring a surge of joy to me just as strong as when I first heard the news, and I lifted her high in my arms with enthusiasm, putting her down again so rapidly when I remembered her condition that she laughed at me.

"We of the Kanala are not delicate." She smiled. "My mother was out riding her dahara when I first showed signs of my arrival into the world."

I grinned back. "Nonetheless," I said, "I will have to make sure you have plenty of protection from now on."

"Treat me like a baby and I'll be off to marry an Argzoon," she threatened jokingly.

My elation began to be clouded again as I thought of the

102

carriers of the Green Death moving so steadily towards Varnal.

She seemed to notice that something was wrong and asked me what it was.

I told her, grimly, simply, trying not to dramatize the situation, though heaven knew it was bad enough.

She nodded thoughtfully when I had finished.

"But what can we do about it?" she said. "We cannot kill them. They are not sane or well – they hardly know they threaten us."

"That is the trouble," I said. "How do we stop them coming to Varnal?"

"There might be one way," she suggested.

"What is that?"

"We could set the Crimson Plain afire – that would deter them, surely?"

"It would be a crime to destroy the Crimson Plain. And, besides, there are towns and villages on it that would suffer."

"You are right," she agreed.

"Moreover," I said, "they have probably already reached the Crimson Plain by now. It will not be long before they arrive at their destination."

"You mean Varnal?"

"Varnal is the city of which they spoke."

Shizala sighed.

I sat down on a chair and leaned on the table next to it, loosening the war-harness I had worn for so long. Something clattered in my pouch and I drew out what had made the noise.

It was the small tube, the complete part of one of the destroyed machines, I'd guessed, that I had picked up in ruined Bagarad.

I placed it on the table, echoing Shizala's sigh.

"In a few days the Green Death will come to Varnal," she mused, "unless something can be done. Something . . ."

"I have sought a means of countering the effects of the plague," I said. "I have sought it for a very long time – across two continents. I do not think it exists."

"There is still hope," she said, trying to keep my spirits up.

I rose and hugged her close. "Thank you," I said. "Yes – there is still a little hope."

The next morning I was in the central hall conferring with my father by marriage, the Bradhi Carnak; his son, Bradhinak Darnad; my wife, the Bradhinaka Shizala; and my friend the Bradhi Hool Haji. I, the Bradhinak Michael Kane, completed this royal gathering.

Our royal minds seemed incapable of constructive thought as we debated the problem of the Green Death.

I clung to my principles, though it was difficult when my wife and unborn child were being threatened.

"We cannot kill them," I repeated. "It is not their fault. If we kill them we kill something in ourselves."

"I understand you, Michael Kane," said old Carnak, nodding his massive head in agreement. "But what else can we do if Varnal is to be made safe from the Green Death?"

"I think we shall have to come to the decision in the end, Michael Kane," said Hool Haji seriously. "I can see no alternative."

"There has to be an alternative."

"There are five minds trying to think of one," Darnad pointed out. "Five good minds, too – and not one of them has come up with a constructive idea. We could try capturing them – something like that."

"But that would mean coming in physical contact with them and risking the plague ourselves," said Hool Haji. "Thus we should defeat our object."

"We could use some kind of big net to trap them," said Shizala. "Though I suppose that is an impractical idea."

"Indeed, it probably is." Carnak frowned. "But it *is* an idea, my dear."

They were all looking at me. I shrugged. "My mind is as empty as anyone's could be," I said.

Darnad sighed.

"There is only one thing to do, you know, Michael Kane."

"What is that? Not to kill them – I must resist that solution."

"We must go out in our airship and try to persuade them to turn back again," he said.

104

I agreed. It was about the only sensible thing we could do now.

So, soon afterwards, we had taken the air again – Hool Haji, Darnad and myself.

It was not long before we had sighted the rabble, pouring raggedly across the Crimson Plain. It seemed, too, that they had taken on some extra numbers, perhaps folk from some of the villages they had passed through.

Green-tainted faces looked up as we began to drop towards them. They stopped moving and waited.

I used the megaphone to address them again.

"People of the Green Death," I shouted. "Why do you not stay where you are? Have you thought that you might be wrong?"

"You are the one who spoke to us yesterday," came a voice. "You must speak with the mechanic now. It is he who leads us to the ultimate non-functioning!"

The crowd backed away from a man with a green-ravaged face and large, insane eyes. He seemed to resemble in some ways the physician we had originally met in Cend-Amrid.

"Are you the leader?" I asked.

"I am the mind, they are the hands, the motor – all the parts of the moving machine."

"Why do you lead them?"

"Because it is my place to lead."

"Then why do you lead them to other settlements, towns and cities when you know that you will spread the plague wherever you go?"

"It is the benefits I bring them – the benefits of death, the release from life, the ultimate non-functioning."

"Have you no thought for those you infect?"

"We bring them peace," he replied.

"Please do not go to Varnal," I urged. "They do not want your peace – they only want their own."

"Our peace is the one peace – the ultimate non-functioning."

It was obviously still impossible to break through the man's insanity. It would take a subtler psychologist than myself even to begin.

"Do you realize that there are those in Varnal who speak

of destroying you because of the threat you offer?" I asked him.

"Destroy us and we shall not function. That is good."

There was no way round it. The man was totally mad.

With heavy hearts we returned to Varnal.

In the City of the Green Mists – soon to be renamed City of the Green Death, I reflected, if the rabble continued its march – we sat beside the green lake and again tried to resolve our problem.

Darnad was frowning as if searching mentally for a forgotten piece of information.

Suddenly he looked up. "I have heard of one man who might have the skill to devise a cure for the Green Death," he said. "Though I believe the man is a legend – he might not even exist."

"Who is he?" I asked.

"His name is Mas Rava. He was once a physician at the court of Mishim Tep, but he became afflicted with philosophical notions and went off to the mountains somewhere in the far South. Mas Rava had studied all the old Sheev texts he could find. But something turned him into a contemplative and he was never seen again."

"When was he supposed to have been at the court of Mishim Tep?" I asked.

"More than a hundred years ago."

"Then he could be dead."

"I am not sure. I never listened very carefully to the stories about him in Mishim Tep. But one thing I remember – they say he had given himself immortality."

"There is a slim chance that he still exists, however," I said.

"Just a slim one, yes."

"But the chances of finding him are even slimmer in the time we have at our disposal," Carnak pointed out.

"We could never find him in time, whatever happened," Hool Haji said.

Shizala said nothing. She simply bowed her head and looked into the waters of the green lake.

Suddenly there came a cry from behind us and a Pukan-

Nara – which was the name used on Vashu for a leader of a detachment of warriors – came rushing towards us.

"What is it?" I asked him.

"One of our scouting airships has returned," he said.

"Well?" Carnak asked.

"The rabble is moving with unnatural rapidity. They will be at the walls of Varnal within a day."

Darnad glanced at me. "So soon?" he said. "I would never have suspected it. By talking to them we seem to have done ourselves a disservice."

"They are running," the Pukan-Nara said. "From what the scout says, many drop exhausted or dead, but the rest *run*. Something is causing them to rush towards Varnal. We must stop them!"

"We have considered all ways of stopping them," I told him.

"We must fight them."

I clung to my rationality. "We must not," I said wearily, though I was tempted to agree once again.

"Then what can we do?" the Pukan-Nara asked desperately.

I came to the decision that had always really been there.

"I know what this means to you," I said. "It means the same to me – perhaps even more."

"What are you going to say, Michael Kane?" asked my lovely wife.

"We must evacuate Varnal. We must let the Green Death have her and must flee towards the mountains."

"Never!" cried Darnad.

But Carnak put a hand on his son's arm.

"Michael Kane has brought us something more valuable than life or even homeland," he said thoughtfully. "He has brought us responsibility to ourselves – and thus to all men on Vashu. His logic is inescapable, his reasons clear. We must do as he says."

"I will not!" Darnad turned to me.

"Michael Kane!" he cried. "You are my brother – I love you as my brother, as a great fighter, a great friend. You cannot mean what you say. Let Varnal be taken over by that rabble – that diseased people! You must be insane!"

"On the contrary," I said quietly. "It is insanity that I fight.

I am striving to remain sane. Let your father tell you – he knows what I mean."

"These are desperate times, Darnad," Shizala said. "They are complicated times. Thus it is so much harder to know the right action to take when action is called for. The people of the Green Death, like the people of Cend-Amrid, are insane. To use violence against them would be to encourage a different kind of insanity in ourselves. I think that is what Michael Kane means."

"It is a great deal of what I mean." I nodded. "If we give in to fear now, what will the Karnala become?"

"Fear! But is not flight cowardice?"

"There are varieties of cowardice, my son," said Carnak, rising. "I think that flight from Varnal – even though we are strong enough easily to defeat that rabble advancing upon us – is not so great a cowardice. It is a responsibility."

Darnad shook his head. "I still do not understand. Surely there is nothing wrong in defending our city against aggression."

"There are different kinds of aggressors," I said. "There were the Blue Giants of the Argzoon who came against Varnal soon after I had arrived on Vashu. These were a folk of comparatively healthy minds. It was a simple thing to fight them off. It was all we could do. But, if violence is used in this case, we lose touch with our whole cause – my whole cause, if you like, though I thought you all shared it. That is to cure the disease at its source; to cure the double disease of body and mind which has infected Cend-Amrid!"

Darnad looked at Hool Haji, who returned his gaze and then looked away. He glanced at his father and his sister. They said nothing.

He looked at me.

"I do not understand you, Michael Kane, but I will try to," he said at length. "I trust you. If we must leave Varnal then we must leave her."

And then Darnad could no longer control the tears that began to course down his face.

108

Chapter Sixteen

THE EXODUS

AND that is why I hope you will understand how a great city, healthy and strong, was left bereft of its population.

Warriors, craftsmen, women and children, left Varnal in an orderly procession, bearing their possessions with them, the airships – both of the Sheev pattern and my own design – drifting above them. Some left, like Darnad, weeping, others puzzled, some thoughtful, but all knowing in their hearts that it was right.

They left Varnal for a few diseased and deluded souls to make what they wanted of it, or take what they wanted of it.

It was the only thing to do.

I am not normally a thoughtful man, as I have told you, but I try to cling to certain principles, no matter how desperate the situation or terrible the threat. Not through any dogmatism but, if you like, from a fear of fear – fear of the actions one takes from fear, the thoughts one deludes oneself with from *fear*.

I rode a dahara, side by side with Shizala on my right and Hool Haji on my left. To his left was Carnak, Bradhi of the Kanala; to Shizala's right was Darnad, stern-faced and puzzled of eye.

Behind us rode or walked the proud folk of Varnal, the graceful city of the Green Mists falling further and further behind us.

Ahead were bleak mountains which we would make our home until some hope could be found for those smitten by the Green Death.

It was not merely the physical fate of Mars that was at stake as we made our exodus from the city. It was the moral fate – the psychological fate. We left Varnal so that Mars might still remain the planet I loved and Varnal itself might remain the city where I felt most at home.

We fought against fear and against hysteria and against the dreadful, insane violence that these emotions bring.

We did not leave Varnal to set an example to others. We left in order to set an example to ourselves.

All this may sound grandiose. I only ask that you consider what we did and try to understand its objectives.

Our journey to the mountains was a long one, for our pace was set by our slowest citizen.

At last the cold mountains were reached and we found a valley where we could build crude houses for ourselves, since the sides of the valley were thickly wooded.

This done, we set off in our airships to explore the mountains in the hope that we should find the almost legendary physician who was, perhaps, the only man on Mars who could save our world from the Green Death.

It was not I who eventually found Mas Rava, but he who had first named him – Darnad.

Darnad came back to the camp one night in his airship. He had taken to travelling alone and we sympathized with the necessity he felt for this.

"Michael Kane," he said, entering the cabin where Shizala and I now lived. "I have seen Mas Rava."

"Can he help us?" was my first question.

"I do not know. I did not speak to him, save to ask him his name."

"That is all he told you?"

"Yes. I asked who he was and he replied, 'Mas Rava'."

"Where is he?"

"He is living in a cave many *shatis* from here. Do you wish me to take you to him?"

"I think so," I replied. "Do you think he has become a complete hermit? Will he be affected by our plight?"

"I cannot tell. In the morning I will take you there."

So, in the morning, we left in Darnad's airship to find Mas Rava. Just as I had earlier sought the machines in the hope that they would save us, now I sought a man. Would the man prove more helpful than the machines? I was not sure. Should I have trusted the machines so much? Should I have trusted another man so much? Again I was not sure.

But I went with Darnad, navigating the ship amongst the crags, until we came to a place where a natural path climbed a mountain to a cave.

I lowered a ladder on to the wide ledge outside the cave and began to climb down until I stood outside the dark entrance.

Then I walked inside.

A man sat there, his back against the cave wall, one leg crooked and the other straight. He regarded me with humorous and quizzical eyes. He was clean-shaven and quite young looking. The cave was clean and neatly furnished.

He was not my idea of a hermit, nor did his cave resemble a hermit's lair. There was something urbane about the man.

"Mas Rava?" I said.

"The same. Sit down. I had one visitor yesterday, and I was rather rude to him, I'm afraid. He was my first. I am better prepared for my second. What is your name?"

"Michael Kane," I said. "It is a long, complicated story, but I come from the planet Negalu," I told him, using the Martian name for Earth, "and from a time far in your future."

"In that case you are an interesting man for my first real visitor," said Mas Rava.

I sat down beside him.

"Have you come seeking information from me?" was his next question.

"In a way," I said. "But first you had better hear the whole story."

"Make it the whole one," said Mas Rava. "I am not an easy man to bore. Proceed."

I told him everything I have told you, everything I had thought and said, everything that was thought and said to me. It took me several hours, but Mas Rava listened all the time without interrupting.

When I had finished, he nodded.

"You have got yourself and your adopted people into an interesting predicament," he said. "As a physician I am a little rusty, though you were right in one thing. There was a cure for the plague, according to my reading. It was not in the form of a machine – that is where you went wrong – but in the form

111

of a bacteria capable of combating the effects of the Green Death in a mere matter of moments."

"Do you know of any place where I could find a container of this bacteria?" I asked him.

"There are several repositories on Vashu similar to the Yaksha vaults you discovered. It could be in any one of them – though it is likely that something as relatively unimportant to either the Sheev or the Yaksha might easily have been allowed to corrode away."

"So you think there is little chance of finding the antidote?" I asked despairingly.

"Yes, I do," he said. "But you could try."

"And what about you – could you prepare an antidote?"

"In time, I might," he said. "But I do not think I will."

"You would not even attempt it?"

"No."

"Why is that?"

"Because, my friend, I am a convinced fatalist." He laughed. "I am sure that the Green Death will pass and that its passage will leave a mark on Vashu. But I think that mark is necessary to society – particularly a society that knows no deep dangers. It will prevent it stagnating."

"I find your attitude difficult to understand," I said.

"Let me be honest, then, and put it to you in another way. I am a lazy man – indolent. I like to sit in my cave and think. I think, incidentally, on a very high plane. I am also a man who needs little company. I have my fear, too, if you like – but it is a fear of becoming involved with humanity and thus losing myself. I value my individuality. So I rationalize all this and I become a fatalist. I have no concern with the affairs of the inhabitants of this planet, or any other planet. It is *planets* that interest me – not *a* planet."

"It would seem to me, Mas Rava," I said quietly, "that you, in your own way, have lost your sense of perspective just as much as the rulers of Cend-Amrid."

He thought over this statement and then looked into my face with a grin.

"You are right," he said.

"Then you will help us?"

"No, Michael Kane, I will not. You have taught me a lesson and it will be of interest to speculate on what you have said. But I will not help you. You see" – he grinned at me again – "what I have just realized, without bitterness or despair, is that I am essentially a stupid man. Perhaps the Green Death will come my way, eh?"

"Perhaps," I said in disappointment. "I am sorry you will not help us, Mas Rava."

"I am sorry, too. But think of this, Michael Kane, if the words of a stupid man mean anything to you . . ."

"What is that?"

"The wish is sometimes enough," said Mas Rava. "Keep wishing that you might find the Green Death gone – provided you keep acting as well, even if you do not understand your own actions."

I left the cave.

Patiently, Darnad was still there, the rope-ladder still touching the ledge.

With a feeling of puzzled curiosity rather than disappointment, I climbed back into the cabin.

"Will he help us?" Darnad asked eagerly.

"No," I told him.

"Why not? He must!"

"He says he will not. All he told me was that a cure for the plague did exist, might possibly exist now – and it is not a machine."

"Then what is it?"

"A container of bacteria," I mused. "Come on, let us return to the camp."

Next day I had made up my mind to return to Varnal and see what had happened to the city.

I took an airship without saying where I was going.

Varnal looked unchanged – even more beautiful, if anything – and as I landed in the city square there was no smell of death as I had expected, and none of the subtler smell of fear.

I stayed in my cabin, however, for safety's sake, and called out through the empty streets.

In a little while I heard footsteps and a woman with a small child walked round the corner. The woman was an upstanding person and her child looked very healthy.

"Who are you?" I asked in astonishment.

"Who are *you* is more to the point?" she replied boldly. "What are you doing in Varnal?"

"This is the city where I normally live," I said.

"And this is the city where I normally live, too," she said crisply. "Were you one of those who left?"

"If you mean was I one of the many thousands who left the city when the folk with the Green Death came," I said, "the answer is 'yes'."

"All that is over now," she said.

"What is over?"

"The Green Death. I had it for a while, you know."

"You mean you have been cured? How? Why?"

"I don't know. It was coming to Varnal that did it. Maybe that's why we came here. I can't remember the journey too clearly."

"You all came to Varnal and it cured you of the plague? What could it be – the water? The air? Something like that? By the Sheev, surely all my questing has not been for nothing. Surely the answer has not lain here all the time!"

"You sound a bit crazy to me," said the woman. "I don't know what it is. I only know I'm cured – and so's everybody else. A lot of them have gone back home, but I stayed on."

"Where do you originally come from?" I asked.

"Cend-Amrid," she said. "I miss it, rather."

I began to laugh uncontrollably.

"Here all the time!" I yelled. "Here all the time!"

Chapter Seventeen

TO CEND-AMRID

By a strange twist of fortune, it seemed, we were now able to return to Varnal.

It was a joyful occasion and the journey back was swifter even than the journey away from Varnal.

It was not only, of course, because of this that we felt light-hearted. We had discovered a cure for the plague – or, at least, we had discovered that the plague could be cured.

Once we had settled in Varnal, to the surprise of the few people who had made the city their home, we began to inspect the damage. There was nothing serious save that anything vaguely mechanical had been hurled into the green lake.

This must have been part of the mob's insane urge to destroy anything 'functional'.

Now it struck me that something could have been thrown into the lake that had caused the water to turn into an antidote for the plague.

I tried to think what it might be.

But I could not. Only now can I look back and wonder if that small tube I had carried with me from Bagarad, and which I never found again, had contained the antidote.

I shall never know.

The important thing is that the water of the Lake of the Green Mists was now able to combat the plague, and all we needed to do was to get it into containers and carry it to the victims.

This became our most important task.

We designed tanks to hold the green water and devised a means of attaching them to our airships.

Then we set off towards the central source of the plague – the insane city of Cend-Amrid.

With us we took Ala Mara, whom I had seen little of since she had rescued us, but who had begged to return with us.

115

A fleet of airships – all that we could muster – began the journey and our hopes were high. We flew away from Varnal with its pennants fluttering bravely from her towers again, towards the horror of the plague.

In the leading airship were myself, Hool Haji and Ala Mara. In the nearest one to us was Darnad and his men, and behind us came the airships in charge of Varnala's bravest Pukan-Naras.

At several points we discovered towns and villages where the plague raged and were able to dispense the small amount of water needed to cure it.

Finding so many places infected, we concentrated first on helping these, and thus it was some time before we sighted Cend-Amrid ahead of us. It was the source of the plague and now, thanks to the green water, it was the last place where the plague flourished.

We came cautiously to the city and hovered above its houses.

Then we drifted until we were over the Central Place, the squat, ugly building where dwelt the Eleven.

Wooden-stepped and walking more stiffly and slower than when I had last observed and fought his kind, a guard appeared on the roof.

With immobile face he looked up.

"Who you? What want?"

"We bring a cure for the Green Death," I told him.

"No cure."

"We have one."

"No cure."

"Tell the Eleven that we bring a cure. Tell the Eleven to come to us."

"I tell."

The man walked stiffly off. It was hard to believe that a human being still lived under the robot-like exterior, but I was sure one could be found.

Soon the Eleven came on to the roof – though I was astonished to count Twelve of them.

Looking closely at their expressionless faces I could see that one of them was Barane Dasa, the man we had met in prison,

"Barane Dasa!" I cried. "What are you doing back with these people?"

He did not reply.

"You," I said pointing. "Barane Dasa! Answer me!"

The blank face remained expressionless.

"I One," came the cold voice.

"But you – they judged you insane."

"Mind repaired."

I shuddered to think what that phrase might imply – even crude brain surgery was suggested by the statement 'mind repaired'.

"What want Cend-Amrid?" said another of the council.

"We bring a cure for the Green Death."

"No cure."

"But there is one – we have it – we have proved it."

"Logic prove no cure."

"But I can illustrate the fact that we have a cure," I said desperately.

"No cure."

I rolled down the ladder. I was going to have to talk to these fear-created creatures face to face, hope that a little humanity could be touched in them.

"Lower the water tank," I said to Hool Haji. "Perhaps that will convince them."

"Be careful, my friend," he warned.

"I will be," I said. "But I do not think they will use physical violence themselves."

Soon I was standing on the flat roof, addressing the Eleven.

"Why do you call yourselves 'Eleven' still?" I asked. "You are Twelve again."

"We Eleven," they said, and I could not shake them. Evidently they had gone ever further down the road to unreality than when I had first met them.

I stared into the cold, blank faces, looking for some sign of real life there, but I could find none.

Suddenly one of the Eleven pointed upwards.

"What that?"

"You've seen one before. It's an airship."

"No."

117

"But you saw one when I last came to Cend-Amrid!"

"What that?"

"An airship – they fly through the air. I showed you how the motor worked."

"No."

"But I did!" I said, exasperated.

"No. Airship not possible."

"But of course they are possible. There it is for your own eyes. It exists!"

"Airship not work. Idea of airship non-functional idea."

"You fools. You can see one working in front of you. What have you done to your own minds!"

One of the Eleven now put a whistle to his lips and blew a shrill note.

On to the roof the sword-wielding automatons who served them came running.

"What is all this about?" I asked. "You must realize we are here to help you."

"You make Cend-Amrid Machine non-functional. You destroy principle – you destroy motor – you destroy machine."

"What principle?"

"The First Idea."

"The idea that drove you to become what you are? What motor?"

"You are not a motor – you are individual human beings. What machine?"

"Cend-Amrid!"

"Cend-Amrid is not a machine – it is a city created and lived in by people."

"You make unfactual statement. You be made non-functional."

Unwillingly, I drew my sword, but it was all I could do. From above I heard a great yell from Hool Haji followed by a thump as he leapt from the airship and landed beside me.

The Eleven instructed their guards to attack us.

The great press of automatons came towards us, raising their swords as one man.

Close to the edge of the roof, it seemed that Hool Haji and

I would be toppled over within a few moments by the sheer mass of the guards.

Then, shouting the ancient cries of the Kanala, Darnad and other Varnalian warriors joined me, leaping from their airships until we formed a thin line of fighting men against the horrible, dead things that came towards us, slowly, at exactly the same pace, like a single strange entity.

The fight began.

The bravery of the Kanala is a legendary thing throughout the whole of Southern Mars, but they were never so brave as in this fight, when the thing they fought seemed never to die.

Every guard that went down was replaced by another. Every sword that was knocked from a fist was substituted by another. We had nothing at our backs but thin air, and so we could not retreat.

Somehow, by sheer will-power I think now, we actually began to gain ground from the automatons.

We pushed them back, our swords flickering and flashing in the light, our battle-cries rarely off our lips as we shouted to one another to keep our spirits up.

Many of the automatons went down.

Not one of our men received more than a minor wound. Somehow we all survived against the might of the men-turned-machines.

But, bit by bit, they surrounded us and crushed us inwards until there was no room to fight.

Then we were captured – not killed, as I had expected – and our swords wrenched from our hands.

What did the Eleven intend to do with us now?

I looked up at our airships. What would they do with those? With the plague-curing water we had brought?

I wondered if there was never to be good health and sanity in Cend-Amrid.

Chapter Eighteen

HOPE FOR THE FUTURE

WE were imprisoned in the same kind of cell we had found ourselves in before.

There were quite a few of us and it was rather cramped. I could not understand why we had not been killed outright, but I decided to accept this and begin trying to think of a means of escape.

I inspected our cell. It had been well made and designed specifically to imprison men – a rare thing on Mars, where the whole idea is normally abhorrent.

Suddenly I remembered the slim dagger that Fasa the cat-girl had given me earlier.

I removed it from my harness and looked at it, wondering how it might be used to our advantage.

There are only so many ways of escaping from prison – if the prison has been thoughtfully designed in order to afford no entrance but the door. I considered them all, going carefully over the door in particular.

The hinges were its weakest point. I began to work at the wood of the door-frame, near the hinges, with the idea of hauling the door inwards.

I must have worked, absorbed in what I was doing for several *shatis*.

At length I had succeeded in cutting the wood away from the frame. Then Hool Haji, Darnad and myself hauled at the door. It groaned inwards, the bar on the other side falling down with a clatter.

No one seemed to have heard us.

Silently, we began to move towards the steps that led up to the first floor of the Central Place.

We had just reached the corridor and were hoping that we could somehow reach the roof and the airships – if they were still there – when I heard a sound to my left.

I whirled, dagger in hand, crouched and ready for action. A figure stood there, blank-faced and stiff-bodied.

"One!" I said. "Barane Dasa!"

"I was coming to cells," came the cold voice. "Now it not necessary. You come."

"Where to?" I asked.

"To main water supply Cend-Amrid," was the reply. "Your tanks are there."

Wonderingly, we followed him, still unsure, still believing this might be some kind of trap.

We followed him through corridors and passages that seemed to lead away from the Central Place, perhaps underground, until we came to a high roofed place that was in semidarkness. Here a great reservoir of water gleamed. On a kind of jetty leading out into the reservoir were the tanks in which we had carried the green water from the Lake of the Green Mists.

Somehow Barane Dasa must have manhandled them here by himself!

"Why do you go against the Eleven?" I asked him, as I checked that the tanks had not been tampered with.

"It is necessary."

"But when I last saw you, you were a fairly normal human being. What has happened to you?"

For an instant his face relaxed and his eyes had a faint, ironic gleam. "To help them we must not attack them," he said. "I think you taught me that, Michael Kane."

I was astonished.

This man had pretended to become 'rehabilitated' into the Eleven so that he could try to reverse the effects of the creed he had himself originated. I could only admire him. I thought he might do it – once the plague was cured for good and all.

"But I still cannot quite see why you brought us here," I said.

"For more than one reason. You saved the life of my niece, Ala Mara, while you were here. That is simple gratitude. But also you showed me how I might best work to correct the crime I began here in Cend-Amrid."

121

I reached out and gripped his arm. "You are a man, Barane Dasa, You *will* do it."

"I hope so. Now you must all get the antidote into the water supply. All machines need fuel," he said, "and the machines of Cend-Amrid must drink."

His reasoning was sound. We were going to do good, as he hoped to do personally, by stealth.

Soon we had got all the green water into the reservoir and our work was done – or would be done in the course of a day.

Now Barane Dasa said, "You come," returning to his original rôle.

We followed him through a series of winding passageways.

Slowly we began to work our way higher and higher until, to my astonishment – for I had completely lost my bearings – we found ourselves on the roof of the Central Place.

And there were our airships.

They were in exactly the place we had left them.

Peering down from the cabin of my own airship was Ala Mara, a smile of relief on her face.

"Uncle!" she whispered excitedly when she saw Barane Dasa. But the man did not look at her, keeping his face rigid and his body straight. He did not even make a gesture to her.

"Uncle" – her voice broke a little – "don't you recognize me – Ala Mara, your niece?"

Barane Dasa remained silent.

I made a sign for her – a gesture that was meant to comfort her, but I heard her sob as she retreated into the cabin.

"Why did they do nothing to our airships?" I said softly to Barane Dasa.

"Airships not exist," he said.

"So they cannot see them – or have deluded themselves into thinking that they can't see them."

"Yes."

"You have a hard fight on your hands for one man," I said.

"Plague gone – fight easier," he said. "Plague go fast – this take longer."

"And you will win, if any man can," I said, voicing the sentiments I had expressed earlier.

122

I gripped his arm once more and began to climb the ladder up to the cabin. I would need to comfort Ala Mara now, tell her a little at least of what her uncle had been forced to make of himself.

Soon we were all swinging up the ladders and entering our cabins.

Our main mission had been a success and some of our earlier exhilaration had returned.

The airships swung in the air, pointing back towards Varnal.

Soon we were speeding rapidly over the lakes, crossing the place of flowers and quicksands.

We were going home. In a sense we were already there, for our hearts were at ease and our minds at rest at long last!

We came back to Varnal on a peaceful morning full of gentle sunlight. The green mists swirled delicately through the city, the marble towers gleamed and glinted, and the whole city scintillated with light like a precious gem.

Far away came a faint sound, as of children singing, and we knew we were hearing the songs of the Calling Hills.

The whole of Mars seemed at peace. We had fought long and hard for that peace, but we were not heroes because of that. All we had done, in a sense, was to make heroes of all those who had fought with us.

It was enough.

Shizala was waiting in the central square near the palace. She was mounted on the broad back of a gentle dahara and she had another beast saddled and ready beside her.

I was not tired and I knew that she would know that.

I was quick to scramble down the ladder and swing from it on to the back of the waiting dahara.

I leant over and kissed my wife, hugging her close to me.

"Is it over?" she asked.

"Mainly," I said. "In time it will be nothing but a memory of sadness and disturbance. It is good that Vashu should have such memories."

"Yes." She nodded. "It is good. Come – let us ride to the Calling Hills as we used to when we first met."

Together we urged our daharas forward through the quiet

morning, riding through the lovely streets and out towards the Calling Hills.

With my beautiful wife riding beside me, and with the exhilaration of the fast ride, I knew that I had won something of immense value – something that I might well have lost if I had not come to Mars as I did.

The cool scents of the Martian autumn in my nostrils, I gave myself up to the joy that comes from true and simple happiness.

EPILOGUE

I HAD listened with keen interest to Michael Kane's story and it had moved me to a deeper emotion than any I had experienced before.

Now I realized why he seemed so much more relaxed than he had ever been before. He had found something – something rare on Earth.

At that point I was tempted to ask him to let me return to Mars with him, but he smiled.

"Would you really like that?" he asked.

"I – I think so."

He shook his head.

"Find Mars in yourself," he said. Then he grinned. "It is far less strenuous, for one thing."

I thought this over and then shrugged.

"Perhaps you're right," I said. "But at least I'll have the pleasure of committing your story to paper. So others will have the pleasure of sharing a little of what you found on Mars."

"I hope so," he said. He paused. "I suppose you think me rather sentimental."

"What do you mean?"

"Well, trying to describe all my emotions to you – the bit I told you about our ride to the Calling Hills."

"There is a great difference between sentimentality and honest sentiment," I told him. "The trouble is that people tend to confuse one for the other and so reject both. All we seek is honesty."

"And an absence of fear." He smiled.

"That comes with honesty," I suggested.

"Partly," he agreed.

"What a mistrusting lot we are on Earth," I said. "We are so blind that we even distrust beauty when we see it, feeling that it cannot be what it appears to be."

"A healthy enough feeling," Kane pointed out. "But it can,

as you say, go too far. Perhaps the old medieval ideal is not such a bad one – moderation in all things. So often that phrase is taken to apply to just the physical side of mankind, but it is just as important to his spiritual development, I think."

I nodded.

"Well," he said. "For fear of boring you further, I will return to the basement and the matter transmitter. I find that Earth is a better place every time I return – but I find Mars the same, also. I am a lucky man."

"You are an exceptionally lucky man," I said. "When will you come back? There must be more adventures yet to come."

"Wasn't that one enough?" He grinned.

"For the moment," I told him. "But I will soon want to hear more."

"Remember," he joked, pretending to wag a warning finger. "Moderation in all things."

"It will comfort me as I wait for your next visit," I said, smiling.

"I will be back," he assured me.

And then he had left the room – left me sitting beside a dying fire, still full of memories of Mars.

There would be even more memories for me soon. Of that I was sure.

NEL BESTSELLERS

NEL BESTSELLERS

NEL P.O. BOX 11, FALMOUTH, CORNWALL

Please send cheque or postal order. Allow 5p per book to cover postage and packing (Overseas 6p per book).

Name ....

Address ....

....

....

Title ....